DON'T LOOK DOWN

"If you touch your gun, Ben," Clint said, "I'll have to kill you."

"Hey, cow pie," Ricks said to Clint. "In case you haven't noticed, I have a gun on you."

"It doesn't matter," Clint said. "I can draw and fire before you pull the trigger."

"Can't be done," Ricks said.

"It can."

"How do you know?"

"You should have shot me in the back," Clint said, "but you didn't. Do you know why?"

"Why?"

"Because you think you can take me," Clint said. "Oh, not fair and square, but you think that havin' your gun out gives you an edge. Well, it doesn't."

"You're bluffin'."

"Pull the trigger then," Clint said. "Go ahead—but when you do, don't look at your gun."

"Wha—" Ricks said, and looked at his gun for just a split second . . .

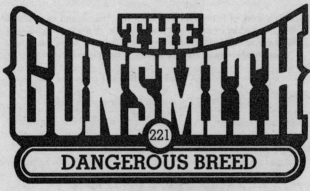

THE GUNSMITH

221

DANGEROUS BREED

J. R. ROBERTS

JOVE BOOKS, NEW YORK

DANGEROUS BREED

A Jove Book / published by arrangement with
the author

PRINTING HISTORY
Jove edition / May 2000

All rights reserved.
Copyright © 2000 by Robert J. Randisi.
This book may not be reproduced in whole or in part,
by mimeograph or any other means, without permission.
For information address: The Berkley Publishing Group,
a division of Penguin Putnam Inc.,
375 Hudson Street, New York, New York 10014.

The Penguin Putnam Inc. World Wide Web site address is
http://www.penguinputnam.com

ISBN: 0-515-12809-0

A JOVE BOOK®
Jove Books are published by The Berkley Publishing Group,
a division of Penguin Putnam Inc.,
375 Hudson Street, New York, New York 10014.
JOVE and the "J" design
are trademarks belonging to Penguin Putnam Inc.

PRINTED IN THE UNITED STATES OF AMERICA

10 9 8 7 6 5 4 3 2 1

ONE

Clint Adams reined in the unruly horse he was riding and dismounted. Not only was the big Morgan unruly, he was stubborn. He walked the animal back to the corral, removed his saddle and brought it into the livery, then returned to the house.

Ever since he had been forced to put his big black gelding, Duke, out to pasture he'd been trying to find a replacement. He'd ridden a dozen horses since then. Not that he expected any horse to live up to Duke, but none of them had even come close to being acceptable.

"That gelding has ruined you for life for any other horse," his friend Art Dwyer said from his chair on the porch. Dwyer was a Wyoming horse breeder who was trying to help Clint find a replacement.

Clint walked over and sat in a chair next to his friend, who handed him a glass of iced tea his wife had prepared.

"Thanks." Clint took a sip and put the sweating glass down on the floor next to his chair.

"Your standards are too high, Clint," Dwyer said.

"Ain't no horse gonna be able to live up to them."

"I'm not asking for much, Art," Clint said.

"You just want an animal who can run like the wind, run all day, is smart, proud, a little stubborn but not too stubborn, broke but not broken and . . . what else?"

"That'll do."

Dwyer shook his head.

"Ain't a horse like that alive."

"Duke is still alive."

"Other than Duke."

"You got that right."

"Then you gotta lower your sights."

"Maybe I just have to keep looking."

"Do you know a better horse breeder than me?"

"No."

"Then where else you gonna look?" Dwyer asked. "You just leave it to me, I'll find you an animal."

"I'm counting on you, Art."

Clint picked up his iced tea and drank down half of it. Dwyer's wife, Ramona, came out onto the porch at that point with a fresh pitcher.

"Freshen that for you?" she asked.

"You're an angel from heaven, Ramona," Clint said, holding his glass up for her to refill.

"Dinner will be ready soon," she said. "I hope you're both hungry."

"Starved," Clint said.

"My belly is stuck to my back," Dwyer said.

"Fifteen minutes," Ramona said, and then went back inside.

Clint looked at his friend's hawklike profile.

"I know what you're thinkin'," Dwyer said. "How'd a ugly old coot like me get so lucky."

"Maybe I was thinking that Ramona was a lucky woman," Clint said.

"Liar!"

"Yeah, you're right," Clint said. "I was thinking what you said."

"Everybody thinks that," Dwyer said. "She's fifteen years younger than me and beautiful. To tell you the truth, I don't know what I did to get so lucky, and I don't care. I'm just glad that I am."

Clint looked out over his friend's operation. Not one of the largest in Wyoming, but certainly one of the best. Dwyer supplied horses to the army, the Rangers, to various stagelines, and even to some western shows. The man's abilities with a horse were uncanny. He could do more with the tone of his voice than most other breeders and trainers could do with their hands. This was the reason Clint decided—after fruitless months of searching for a replacement for Duke—that he had to come to Wyoming to let Art Dwyer set him up with another horse.

He'd been at Dwyer's a week, though, and his old friend had not been able to pair him up with a suitable mount yet. The man was beginning to take it as a challenge, though, and Clint wasn't quite ready to move on.

"We better get inside for dinner," Dwyer said, hoisting himself from his chair, "or she'll throw it out."

Dwyer was tall and almost painfully thin, with hair he wore long and usually tied back. He looked like he had Indian blood, but Clint knew he didn't. It was the nut-brown skin that did it, a result of so many hours spent in the sun over the years, and the sharp profile.

Clint stood up without being told again. He had already gained a healthy respect for Ramona's cooking.

"Tell the truth," Dwyer said. "When you got here and

found me with Ramona, you were shocked, weren't you?"

"Truthfully, yes," Clint said, "but not for the reasons you think."

"Then why?" Dwyer asked. "If not because she's too beautiful and classy for me."

"I was surprised," Clint said, "that you had finally found a woman who would put up with you."

"Well," Dwyer said, putting his hand on Clint's shoulder, "not only does she put up with me, she's made me a better man. I don't drink as much, and I sure don't whore around no more because she'd geld me if she found out, and she's one hell of a cook."

"Yeah," Clint said, looking his friend's spare frame up and down, "I can see she's putting the pounds on you."

"You said it," Dwyer said. "Why, I had to let my belt out a notch after we was married two months."

Clint looked at his friend's belt, which still had plenty of notches left.

"Yep," Clint said, "I can see where she's making you fat as a house, Art."

TWO

Two men watching the Dwyer spread from the safety of a nearby hill observed the two men—Dwyer and his guest—stand up and walk into the house about ten minutes after Ramona Dwyer.

"So, when are we goin' down?" Ben Gunner asked.

Hal Ricks ignored him and kept staring down the hill.

"Ain't she pretty?" he asked then.

"She's real pretty, Hal," Gunner said, "but I don't know if she's gonna be worth all this troub—"

Gunner's words were cut off when Ricks' hand closed around his throat. The strength in the man's hand was tremendous and Gunner could not get any air, at all.

"I tol' you before, Ben, to watch what you say about her, didn't I?" Ricks asked.

It took a few moments before he realized that Gunner could not answer him with his throat closed. He opened his hand and his friend took in huge gulps of air.

"Didn't I?"

"Yeah," Gunner said, between gulps, "you did, Hal, you surely did."

"Good," Ricks said, and looked down the hill again.

"So, when *are* we goin' in, Hal?"

"Soon as the rest of the boys get here, Ben," Ricks said. "Just sit back and relax a while. They'll be here soon enough."

THREE

After dinner Clint and Art Dwyer found themselves back out on the porch again, this time each holding a cup of Ramona's coffee.

"Somebody up on the hill," Clint said.

"I see 'em," Dwyer said.

"Not worried?"

"Rustlers, probably."

"Still not worried?"

"They'll watch for a while, see that I've got enough men to fight 'em off, and then move on to somebody else's spread. Happens all the time."

"You warn your neighbors?"

"I pass the word," Dwyer said, "but mostly I just worry about me and mine and what's mine. That's pretty much how everybody around here operates."

Clint looked up the hill. Best he could tell there were two men there, one of them with something that was reflecting the sun—a belt buckle, a nickel-plated gun, maybe a spy glass of some kind.

"Don't worry about them, Clint," Dwyer said. "Drink your coffee. Pretty good, huh?"

Actually, the only thing Clint didn't like about Ramona was her coffee, but he didn't say so.

"It's fine," he said.

"What do you know?" Dwyer asked good-naturedly. "If coffee ain't strong enough to take the finish off yer gun you don't like it."

"It's fine, Art."

"And her cookin'?" Dwyer asked. "Is that fine, too?"

"That's better than fine, and you know it."

"Ya know," Dwyer said, "I never thought I was the kind of man who could fall in love, Clint. For me it was always just whores whenever I got the itch, but this . . . this is more than just satisfying an itch."

"Love usually is, Art."

"Yeah," Dwyer said, "it is."

They finished their coffee on the porch, then went inside to play some two-handed poker for toothpicks. Ramona didn't like gambling, but she put up with that much.

Clint took one last look up the hill before they went inside, but it was getting dark and he couldn't see anything of the men on the hill. His only consolation was, they couldn't see anything, either.

FOUR

The next afternoon Clint decided to take a ride into Two Forks, the nearest town to Art Dwyer's ranch. Dwyer loaned him a horse, a gelded steeldust he thought Clint might like.

"Just ride him to town and back and then make up your mind," he said. "Okay?"

"I'll give him a try, Art."

"And keep an open mind."

"I always do."

"Yeah, right," Dwyer said. "He ain't Duke, Clint. Ain't no other horse ever gonna be Duke."

"I know that."

"Yeah, I know you do," Dwyer said, "but you hold it against them."

Clint decided not to argue the point.

"I'll be back in time for dinner," he said.

"I'll tell Ramona."

Clint mounted the steeldust, waved and rode off. He looked up the hill where the two men had been the day before, but didn't see anyone. He thought about riding up there to check it out, but decided against it.

He would regret that decision for the rest of his life.

Ricks and Gunner waited for Clint Adams—who was a stranger to them at this point—to ride off toward town before resuming their places on the hilltop again. Behind them were four other men who had arrived late last night in Two Forks, and who had ridden out here early that morning.

"He's leavin'," Gunner said. "That's good. One less man to worry ourselves about."

"I wasn't worried," Ricks said.

"I know, Ray," Gunner said, "but I was."

"You worry too much, Ben."

"I'd just like to know who that fella is, that's all."

"It don't matter, now," Ricks said. "He's gone."

"But we don't know how long he'll *be* gone," Gunner pointed out.

"Long enough," Ricks said. "You just get the boys ready to move."

"Sure, Ricks," Gunner said, "sure."

Gunner moved down off the hilltop to face the other men.

"He's doin' all this for a woman?" Clell Miller asked.

"Yeah," Gunner said, "for a woman."

"Don't make no sense," Miller said. "There's plenty of women around."

"According to him," Gunner said, "not like this one."

"A woman is a woman," Miller said. "Long as they're warm and wet."

"And willing?" Gunner asked.

"Naw," Miller said, "ain't got to be willin'."

"You're a pig, Clell."

"Yup," Miller said, "jest like my daddy afore me."

"Get the men ready," Gunner said.

Clint rode into Two Forks, thoroughly disgusted with the horse he was riding. He'd tried a few simple maneuvers, the kind of stuff Duke used to do in his sleep, and the horse had balked. No, this was not the one.

He rode up in front of the saloon and dismounted, remembering to tie the horse to the hitching post tightly—something that had not been necessary with Duke. He went inside and approached the bar. The bartender's name was Eddie. They had made acquaintances during his first day in town, before he moved out to stay with the Dwyers.

"Beer?" Eddie asked.

"You remember. I'm flattered."

"I got a good memory," the man said, setting the beer down in front of him. "For instance, I remember you're looking for a new horse. Find one?"

"Not yet," Clint said sourly.

"Almost like tryin' to find the right woman, ain't it?" Eddie asked, leaning on the bar.

"Worse," Clint said, "much worse. What's been going on here?"

"Nothin' much," Eddie said. "A few strangers in and out. Oh yeah, had three ride in yesterday. Hardcases."

"Still here?" Clint asked, just out of idle curiosity.

"Naw, rode out this mornin'," Eddie said.

Which meant that Clint did not have to worry about one of them jumping out from an alley to try him out. Sometimes Clint felt like the local law again, keeping track of strangers' comings and goings.

"Must be a bitch havin' to jump shadows all the time," Eddie said. He had known who Clint was at first sight, which had not surprised Clint. Bartenders were notoriously well informed, as a group.

"I'd say you get used to it," Clint said, "but you never do."

"What brings you to town?"

"Just stretching my legs," Clint said, "getting some air. You know, even when you stay with someone as a guest the walls can start to close in on you. Just goes to show that you're not ready to settle down yet."

"Which means," Eddie said, "that you still need to find yourself a new horse."

"And," Clint said, pushing his empty beer mug across the bar, "another beer."

FIVE

After the saloon Clint stopped in to see the sheriff, a man with the colorful name Tom Champagne. They'd also met his first day in town, because Clint had stopped in to make a courtesy call and had ended up explaining his reasons for being there. Since then they had talked several more times and had even shared a meal.

Champagne was a few years younger than Clint, shorter and stockier, and had been sheriff of Two Forks for about five years. Clint had the feeling that the man would be there many more years, as he seemed fairly settled into his job.

"Find that horse yet?" the sheriff asked as Clint entered his office.

"Not yet," Clint said. "Is that coffee I smell?"

"Help yourself."

As it happened, Tom Champagne's coffee was better than Ramona Dwyer's. It was strong and was the closest Clint could come to trail coffee while in Two Forks. Right now trail coffee was the only thing he was missing about being on the trail.

Clint retrieved one of several cups that were hanging from nails on the wall surrounding the cell keys, which were always on the center nail. He took his coffee and sat down across from the lawman.

"Any company?" he asked.

"Cells are empty," Champagne said. "It was a quiet night, although I was expectin' some fireworks."

"Why's that?"

"Three strangers rode in yesterday. Hardcases."

"That's what Eddie told me."

"Looked like the type who'd find trouble even when they wasn't lookin'," Champagne said, "but that didn't turn out to be the case. In fact, while I was over there they seemed to be on their best behavior."

"And now they're gone?"

"Rode out this morning."

"Any other strangers in town?"

"Like who?"

"Two men together?"

"Anybody particular in mind?"

"Nope," Clint said, "just happened to notice two men watching Art Dwyer's ranch."

"Rustlers, most likely lookin' for a likely spread to hit," Champagne said. "That won't be Art's. He ain't been hit in a while."

"You don't seem any more concerned than he was."

"I ain't," the lawman said. "Folks 'round here know better than to hit Art Dwyer's place."

"I hope you're right."

"I'll pass the information along to some of the other ranchers, though," Champagne said. "Just to keep them on their toes."

"Sounds like a good idea."

"What'd you ride into town today?" Champagne
asked.

"A steeldust," Clint said, making a face, "with a hard
mouth. Won't mind the bit at all . . ."

After talking with Tom Champagne for a while Clint
just walked around town, tipping his hat to the ladies.
There were several attractive, single ladies he'd seen in
town, but since he was staying out at the Dwyer ranch
he'd yet to make the acquaintance of any. There were
also a couple of girls working in the saloon who seemed
likely candidates for a joyful romp, but he'd yet to convince them to indulge free of charge.

It was very clear to him from his time on the Dwyer
ranch that he was far from ready to be put out to pasture
like ol' Duke. Even now he itched to be on a horse—
but not just any horse. He itched to be riding Duke,
sharing a campfire with the big gelding, as he had been
doing for many years. All the while he and Duke had
been together he had never suffered from any kind of
trail loneliness. He'd talk to Duke while they were riding, or while they were camped, and he swore the big
gelding would listen to him, understanding everything
he said. He wasn't going to get that from another
horse—not right away, anyway. That was going to have
to come with time, but so far he hadn't found an animal
he wanted to spend *that* much time around.

He made one complete circle of the town, which took
a while because Two Forks was a nice size. Certainly
not a Laramie or Tucson, but Two Forks was growing.
That was, in part, due to outfits like Art Dwyer's being
in the vicinity. They brought commerce to the town, not
only by patronizing the merchants themselves, but my
bringing others in—as, in Art's case, when the army

came looking for new mounts. They'd stay in the hotels, eat at the restaurants, frequent the small shops like the barber shop and the large ones, like the general store and the local whorehouse.

When he arrived back at the saloon he entertained the idea of going back inside for another beer. Instead, he continued on several stores until he reached the telegraph office. As soon as he walked in the clerk noticed him and stood up.

"Nothin' today, Mr. Adams," he said, cheerfully.

"I'd like to send one," Clint said.

"Sure thing."

The man grabbed a pencil and Clint dictated a message to Rick Hartman, in Labyrinth, Texas. He told Rick he was still in Two Forks, at the Dwyer ranch, and inquired as to how Duke was doing.

"Miss that big horse of yours, don'tcha?" the clerk asked, then he was done.

"More than I can tell you," he said, forgetting the clerk's name.

"Well, Mr. Dwyer'll fix ya up real good," the man said. "Nobody knows horses like him."

"I know that," Clint said. "Thanks. I'll be around in a day or two, probably."

"I'll hold the reply if I get one," the man said, "run it out to the ranch if it seems important."

"Thanks."

Clint left the telegraph office and stopped on the boardwalk outside. He looked up and down the street, found he knew in his head every inch of the place. A definite indication that he had been there too long.

He walked down to the saloon and approached the steeldust, who was ignoring him. He watched the animal tug against the post for a while, then stop. If he hadn't been tied tight he'd be long gone, by now, probably back at the Dwyer ranch—if he was even *that* smart.

Finally, he untied the horse and had to hold him fast so he wouldn't bolt. He jerked on the animal's head, then chided himself for taking his impatience out on the animal. It wasn't the steeldust's fault he wasn't Duke.

He mounted the animal, turned him, and headed out of town at a leisurely pace. No use trying to get more out of it than it was willing to give.

It.

He'd never referred to Duke as "it," but always as "him." Maybe that was how he'd know he found the right horse. When he started thinking of one as "him" again.

SIX

Clint didn't have to get very close to the ranch before he realized something was wrong. The smoke was a dead giveaway. He urged the steeldust into a gallop, getting as much as he could from the animal, and let up only when they reached the ranch. It was the barn that was giving off most of the smoke, but the house was ablaze, too. One side of the corral had been knocked down and the horses were gone.

And there was a man lying on the ground in front of the house.

Clint dismounted and ran to the fallen man, hoping against hope that it wasn't his friend Art Dwyer. When he turned him over, though, it was Dwyer, and he was dead. He'd been shot several times, but from the looks of his face he'd been beaten before that. Clint looked around, searching for Ramona, or for some of Dwyer's men. That was when he saw two more men on the ground, between the corral and the house. He eased his friend's body to the ground and went to check on them, but they were dead as well—shot.

He stood up and looked around some more. Ramona had to be somewhere, or had she run off and escaped the carnage?

Abruptly, he looked up the hill, at the place where the "rustlers" had been watching the place. He remembered now his fleeting thought of riding up there to check them out before going to town and regretted his decision not to do so. It was too much of a coincidence that they would not be involved in this.

He remembered the sheriff's words from earlier in the day, that, "Folks 'round here know better than to hit Art Dwyer's place."

Well, somebody hadn't known better . . .

There was little he could do to fight the fire and, knowing that the smoke would soon bring others running, he simply set about trying to determine if there were any bodies in the burning buildings. As a result he pulled three dead men from the burning barn. He had not, however, been able to get into the house to see if Ramona was still inside. He just hoped that she hadn't been. Or, at least, if she was, that she'd been shot before the fire was started. Burning to death was a horrible way to go.

He had pulled all the bodies away from the flames by the time the first of the neighbors began to arrive. They immediately set about to try and save the house, the smaller of the burning structures, but Clint knew it was too late to save either building.

"Where's Art?" one of the neighbors asked. Clint recognized him as Peter Dexter, the nearest rancher to Dwyer. He had a much tidier-looking operation, but one that was not much bigger.

Clint pointed to the six dead bodies he'd clustered together.

"Dead."

"Oh, no," the man said, shaking his head. "What about Ramona?"

"Can't find her."

Dexter looked at the burning house, which a bucket brigade was now vainly attempting to extinguish.

"Lord," he said, "don't let her be in there."

Clint wholeheartedly endorsed the prayer.

Sheriff Champagne finally arrived, together with a bunch of people from town who had closed their businesses when they figured out whose place had to be on the fire. Soon, the whole town was there, trying to save Art Dwyer's place . . . but for who?

Champagne stood next to Clint, looking down at the six men who'd been shot to death.

"Art and all his men," the lawman said. "These were good boys, Clint. It would take some good boys to do this to them."

"Two on the hill," Clint said, "and three who rode into town yesterday?"

"You think they're connected?" Champagne asked.

"I think," Clint said, with a hard look on his face, "that I'm damn well going to find out."

SEVEN

By the time the rubble had cooled enough for them to go through most of the neighbors and townspeople had gone back where they belonged. Sheriff Champagne had sent the bodies into town to the undertaker's. It was he and Clint who waited to go through the burnt out buildings, looking for Ramona Dwyer.

They didn't find her.

"I don't know if this is good or bad," Tom Champagne said, as they waded out of the wet, burnt leftovers of Art Dwyer's life. "It can mean two things. Either she got away—"

"Or they took her with them," Clint said.

"Right."

Clint looked up the hill.

"What are you thinking?" Champagne asked.

"I want to take a look up on that hill," Clint said. "There might be something up there that will help me find these men."

"Well," Champagne said, "come on, then. Let's go and take a look."

"You coming?" Clint asked.

"I'm with you all the way, Clint," the sheriff said. "Maybe I didn't know Art as long as you, but he was my friend."

Clint nodded and they both mounted up and rode up the hill.

"Five sets of tracks," Clint said. "Three back here, two at the top of the hill. See here? They laid down here to look down at the house."

"I see it."

"Five," Clint said.

"That supports your theory that the three strangers in town were with these two up here."

"So I'm looking for five men."

"We're lookin' for five men," Champagne said.

"Do you have a deputy to leave in charge while you're away?" Clint asked.

"I'll find one," Sheriff Tom Champagne said.

They decided to bury Art Dwyer before they left. They would do that the next day, which gave them time to ask around town about the three strangers. Eddie, the bartender at the saloon, had gotten a good look at them.

"Just three hardcases, like I said," he replied to their question. "Trail-worn clothes, all in their thirties—oh, wait."

"What?" Clint asked.

"Well, one of them wore his gun on his left hip."

"Was he left-handed, or wearing it butt forward for a crossdraw?" Clint asked.

"No," Eddie said, thinking about it, "he was left-handed. Definitely left-handed."

"Okay," Champagne said, "what about the others?"

"Well, one had a scar here." He touched himself high on the right cheek. I don't have that high a cheekbone, but he did. It was right here, about this long." He drew his finger across his face about an inch. "And deep."

"And the third?"

He thought about it, then said, "There was nothing unusual about the third guy."

"Did you hear any of them called by name?"

"No."

"Did they play poker with anyone?" Champagne asked.

"No."

"They just sat together, the three of them?" Clint asked.

"That's right."

"They were sitting together the one time I came in," Tom Champagne said.

"That's right," Eddie said, again, "and they left soon after you did."

"Okay," the sheriff said, "I guess that's—"

"Wait a minute," Clint said. "Did any of the girls go with them?"

"Hey, that's right," Eddie said, "Rachel and Monica went with them."

"Who went with who?" Clint asked.

"I don't know," Eddie said. "The two girls left with the three men. I don't know who ended up with who."

Clint looked at Champagne, who said. "Well, we'll just ask them."

As it turned out the two girls shared a room over the hardware store, so when they knocked on the door they woke both of them up.

"Sheriff? What's going on?" Rachel, the dark-haired one, answered the door.

"Rachel, we need to talk to you and Monica," Champagne said.

"Well, you can't come in." Rachel said. "We're not . . . decent." She pulled her robe tightly around her.

"You look decent," Champagne said.

"Monica sleeps in the buff."

Clint wondered if they had a man, or men, inside.

"Rachel," Champagne said, "are you working now?"

"We live here, Sheriff," she said. "We don't bring men back here."

"It's okay," Clint said. "We can ask the questions right here."

"What questions?"

"Last night you and Monica left the saloon with three men," Champagne said. "We need to know what you know about them."

"Why? What's this about?"

"Art Dwyer and his men were killed today," Clint said, "and his wife is missing. We have reason to believe these three men might have had something to do with it."

"Oh!" she said, her hand going to her mouth. "Poor Ramona."

"You know her?" Clint asked.

"Yes, and I like her," Rachel said. "Poor Ramona, poor Art!"

"Rachel, what do you and Monica know?" Champagne asked.

Instead of answering she called out, "Mon? Come here, quick!"

"I'm naked," Monica's voice called back.

"Pull something on and come here."

Monica was a busty blonde and what she pulled on did not quite cover her. More than half her pear-shaped breasts were showing, and there was seemingly acres of creamy white skin. Both Clint and the sheriff cleared their throats and tried to avert their eyes.

Rachel told Monica what had happened, and she had the same reaction as her friend.

"Who went with who last night?" Clint asked.

"We went to a hotel room with all three of them," Rachel said.

"You didn't, uh, pair up?" Clint asked.

"Sometimes," Monica said, "and sometimes we're just, you know, all together."

"Okay, then," Clint said, "that really doesn't matter. Did they say anything that might have revealed why they were here?"

"No," Monica said, "they only revealed why they were with us."

"Were any names mentioned?" Champagne asked, still trying not to look at Monica's breasts.

"Well . . ." Monica said, and looked at Rachel. "I thought I heard one of them call another one . . . Earl?"

"It might have been Earl," Rachel said.

"What else could it have been?" Clint asked.

"No," Monica said, "it was Earl."

"Anything else?" Clint asked. "Anything at all?"

Both girls thought hard, then shook their heads.

"No other names," Rachel said. "Not that we heard."

"Okay," Champagne said, "okay, we've got *some*-thing to go on, at least. Thanks, girls."

Clint and the sheriff started down the stairs when Monica suddenly burst out the door—and out of her robe. Her big breasts bobbed free, but she didn't seem to notice. Clint and Champagne did, though. They noticed the heavy, pale undersides of her breasts and her rose-colored nipples.

"There was one other thing," she said.

"W—what?" Champagne asked.

"Well, one of them had an odd way of talkin'."

"Like what?" Clint asked.

"Well, when he did something, one of the other men would call him a pig," she said.

"That's it?" the sheriff asked.

"No, let me finish," she said. "They'd call him a pig and he'd say, 'Just like my daddy before me.' "

"No," Rachel said, also coming outside, "it was more like 'jest like my daddy afore me.' "

"That's right," Monica said, "like that." As an afterthought she gathered up her breasts and put them back into her robe . . . sort of.

" 'Jest like my daddy afore me,' " Clint repeated. "Okay, well, thanks, girls. Thanks a lot."

"We hope you catch 'em," Monica said.

Clint had an afterthought about Ramona being with them.

"Girls, one more thing?" he asked.

"What?" Rachel asked.

"How were they with you?"

The two girls looked at each other, and Rachel asked, "You want to know if they were any good?"

"Know, I mean . . . were they rough."

"They *started* to be," Monica said, "but we don't do rough stuff."

"You're thinkin' about Ramona, ain't you?' Rachel asked.

"Yes."

"Well," she said, "I get the feelin' those boys coulda been pretty rough, if we'd let them."

"I see," Clint said. "Well, okay. Thanks."

He went down the rest of the steps to join Tom Champagne as the door at the top closed.

EIGHT

Clint and Tom Champagne went to the saloon for a beer and to talk over what they knew.

"Not a hell of a lot," Clint said.

"It's not that bad," Champagne said. "We got some physical descriptions and a name."

"I want to know about the two on the hill," Clint said. "Were they ever in town?"

"I don't know."

"Were there any strangers between my arrival and the arrival of the other three?"

"Not that I know of."

"Then where did these two men stay?"

"Maybe they camped," Champagne said.

"We don't have time to ride all over kingdom come looking for a cold camp," Clint said.

"So what do you suggest?"

"Maybe," Clint said, "they stayed with someone in the area."

"You mean," Champagne asked, "one of Art's neighbors?"

Clint nodded.

"Can't be."

"Wasn't he competing with anyone?"

"Well, yeah, for some business," Champagne said, "but there was no competition so intense that it would lead to . . . to this."

"Who was his biggest competition?"

"You met him," Champagne said. "In fact, you saw him today."

"Pete Dexter? Is that who you're referring to?"

"That's right," Champagne said. "Pete wants that army contract that Art has—had."

"Enough to kill for it?"

"Six men?" Champagne asked. "I don't think so."

"Maybe we should go and talk to Dexter," Clint said. "We can't leave until after we bury Art in the morning."

"Dexter will be at the burial."

"We might catch him off guard if we go to his house."

"Pete Dexter . . ." the sheriff said, shaking his head. "I can't see it, Clint. I just can't—"

"I can go alone."

"You don't have any authority," the lawman said. "He won't have to talk to you."

"Why wouldn't he?" Clint asked. "Unless he has something to hide."

Champagne was thinking about it.

"This could work, Tom," Clint said. "I'll go alone. He won't be threatened by me, and maybe he'll let something slip."

"Okay," Champagne said, after some more thought, "but tread easy, Clint. Pete Dexter is an important man, around these parts."

"Maybe more important," Clint added, "now that Art Dwyer is dead."

NINE

Clint rode out to the Dexter ranch on the steeldust, his displeasure with the horse forgotten. Now it was simply a form of transportation, and it got him where he wanted to go.

He was greeted with respect by Pete Dexter and shown into the man's study.

"Can I offer you a brandy?" Dexter asked.

"Sure," Clint said. "I could use a drink."

Dexter poured out two and handed Clint a glass. He lowered his bulk into a chair behind his desk. Dexter was a robust man in his fifties who was just beginning to go to fat. His hair and beard, once jet black, were now shot with gray.

"Here's to Art Dwyer," Dexter said, "best damn horseman I ever knew."

"I'll drink to that," Clint said, and did, then setting the glass down on the edge of the man's desk, "but was he a better horseman than you, Mr. Dexter?"

"You've got me wrong, Adams," Dexter said. "I'm not a horseman, I'm a businessman, and horses are my

33

business. But do you see any scars on these hands? Any missing pieces or fingers? I don't work with the animals myself, I have people who do that for me."

"I see."

"Were you thinking I might be jealous of Art?"

"Well, no—"

"Come on, Adams," Dexter said. "You're a smart man. You must know that I benefit from Art's death."

"Do you?"

"I'm sure to get the army contract he had."

"And would you kill him for that?"

Dexter regarded Clint for a few moments, then drank some more of his brandy.

"Why isn't the sheriff here with you?" he asked.

"He didn't have the same questions I did."

"That's because he knows me better than you do," Dexter said. "Art Dwyer was my neighbor, and more than that, he was my friend. I was the first one to arrive when I saw the smoke at his place."

"After me."

"That's true," Dexter said, "but you were already on the way."

"And neither one of us was first," Clint added. "The killers were first."

"Whoever they were."

"There were five of them," Clint said. "We think we have descriptions of three."

"And the other two?"

"They were watching Art's place from a hill," Clint said, "but they weren't staying in town."

"So you think they were staying here?"

"They were staying someplace," Clint said. "Did you have guests, Mr. Dexter?"

"I did not."

"Did you or any of your men see two strangers about?"

"I didn't," Dexter said, "and if my men did they would have said something about it."

Clint stared at his glass, perched on the edge of the desk in front of him.

"I'm not taking offense at any of this, Adams," Dexter said. "Art was my friend, but you and he were friends a lot longer. Ask me anything you want."

Clint didn't have anything else to ask him. Instead, he picked up his glass, finished it, and stood up.

"I'm finished here, Mr. Dexter."

Dexter stood up too, extended his hand.

"Anything I can do, you let me know," he said, as they shook. "Horses, men, money—"

"I'll let you know," Clint said. "The sheriff and I will be leaving tomorrow after we bury Art."

"Find those bastards, Adams," Dexter said. "Find them and bring Ramona back here."

"That's what I intend to do, Mr. Dexter," Clint said. "That's exactly what I intend to do."

TEN

When Clint got back to town he went to the sheriff's office to fill Champagne in on his conversation with Pete Dexter. He did so over a cup of the sheriff's strong coffee.

"So you believed him?"

"For now," Clint said, "until I have some reason not to."

"I told you it wasn't him."

"Yeah, you did." Clint finished his coffee and stood up. "So we'll leave right after the funeral?"

"I'm ready," Champagne said. "I've already arranged for supplies from the general store. We can pick them up any time. What about a pack horse?"

"It'll slow us down," Clint said. "Let's take whatever we can carry in two canvas sacks."

"All right. What are you gonna ride?"

"The steeldust, I guess," Clint said. "I don't have time to look for something else. It'll have to do for now."

"I guess I'll see you at the graveyard tomorrow mornin' then."

"Yup," Clint said. "Check out your weapons tonight, Tom. We don't want any surprises when we catch up to them."

"Will do."

Clint waved and left the office, going back to his hotel to turn in early. Tomorrow was the first day of a manhunt that wasn't going to end until all five men were caught, no matter how long it took.

After Clint Adams left, Pete Dexter locked all the doors to his house, then went into the kitchen. Using a key, he unlocked the doors that led to what used to be a root cellar. It was being used for something else, now.

He descended into the dark, lit a match, and used it to light a storm lamp. The room was bathed in yellow light, and the woman in the corner cringed as he approached her. She couldn't yell because she was gagged and couldn't do more than cringe because she was bound.

"Hello, Ramona," Dexter said, placing his hand on her head. He stroked her black hair, which was still dirty from the fire. She was still beautiful to him, though, despite the dirt and soot and smoke that clung to her.

"Your friend Clint Adams was here," Dexter said, "but I convinced him I had nothing to do with the fire, so he's going to start looking elsewhere. I admit it's a complication having him involved, but by this time tomorrow night he'll be far away from here, tracking five men who will have, by then, split up. It's going to take him forever to catch the five of them."

She glared at him with hatred in her eyes. He stroked her cheek, which only made her eyes flash even more.

"Don't worry," he said, "you'll be able to clean up soon. I have some nice clothes for you to change into, also. I've been building a wardrobe for you all this time, since you chose Art over me and married him. That was something you should never have done, Ramona. You see, I don't take rejection very well, and I certainly don't take losing very well. Now, with Art dead, not only will I have that army contract, but I'll have you, as well."

She tried to say something to him, but it was unintelligible.

"That's okay, honey," he said. "Soon you'll be able to talk, but I'm going to give you a while to decide what you want to say. Once I take the gag off you had better be very careful of what comes out of your mouth, so think very hard about it."

He turned and walked away.

"I have to go now. Would you like me to leave the lamp on for you?"

She didn't respond.

"No? You like the dark?"

In truth she hated the dark, but she wasn't going to give him the satisfaction of answering him, not even with a nod.

"Very well," he said, and blew out the flame on the lamp, throwing the room into complete darkness, except for the light coming from the open door above. He turned, went up the steps, and soon that light was snuffed out, as well.

Clint removed his gunbelt and hung it on the bedpost, then his shirt and boots. He was sitting on the bed that way when there was a knock on the door. He removed the gun from the holster and carried it to the door.

"Who is it?"

"It's Rachel," a woman's voice said, "from the saloon."

He opened the door and the tall, dark-haired woman smiled tentatively at him.

"It's late, Rachel," he said.

"Actually, it's early."

"Well, it's late for me," he said. "I have to get an early start in the morning. Did you remember something else?"

"Actually, I did," she said. "I remembered what good friends you and Art Dwyer were, and I thought that maybe you might want some company instead of being alone tonight."

"Rachel—"

"Don't worry," she said, "it's free—for both of us."

"Both of you?"

She smiled as her friend, Monica, stepped into the doorway, as well.

"We thought we'd help you get through the night," the busty blonde said, "before you got on the trail to-morrow."

"How about it?" Rachel asked. "We can take your mind off . . . well, almost anything."

He hesitated only a moment, then backed up to allow them to enter and said, "I bet you could . . ."

ELEVEN

Each woman took one arm and led Clint to the bed. He returned his gun to his holster before allowing them to sit him down. Once he was seated they proceeded to take off their clothes very slowly, until they were both naked. His eyes widened at the sight of so much female flesh, and his body reacted. Both women were giving off heat and a scent that was pure sex.

Naked, they knelt before him and removed his trousers, and then his underwear so that he was as naked as they were. His penis sprang to attention, fully erect and engorged.

"Oh my, Monica," Rachel said, "look."

"Mmmm," Monica said, "I am looking."

But then they stopped looking and started touching. They each stroked one of his legs, from ankle to thigh, running their hands along his inner thigh, and then—as if they had planned it—one of them took his penis in her hand and stroked it while the other cupped and fondled his testicles.

Rachel had his dick in her hand and then leaned over

to rub it against her cheek. Monica put her hand on his chest to push him down onto his back so they could both get to him easier. Once he was on his back with his legs spread they each went to work.

Rachel worked her lips and tongue up and down his rigid shaft, finally stopped at the spongy head to lick it lovingly before taking the entire length of him into her mouth. She began to suck him wetly while Monica licked his thighs, and his balls, and slid her hand beneath him to cup his ass cheeks.

When Rachel allowed him to slip from her lips Monica was there to take him in again, moving her head up and down, sliding him in and out of her mouth. Meanwhile, Rachel joined him on the bed and pressed her peach sized breasts to his lips. He bit and sucked her nipples while she stroked his chest and ran her hands through his pubic hair while her blonde friend continued to moan and suckle him. She pulled her breasts away from his mouth then and kissed him, sliding her tongue inside.

Abruptly, both women turned him so that he was lying on the bed the long way. Monica mounted him, then, and took his saliva-slickened penis inside of her. He was able to watch her only for a moment, though, before Rachel straddled his face and, facing her friend, brought her fragrant pussy down over his mouth. He reached up to grab her ass and began to lick and suck her while Monica rode him up and down, up and down, up and down . . .

Then Monica was off him, his penis chilled because it was so wet. Rachel moved away from him also, and he realized they were going to switch places. In moments he was buried inside of Rachel's steamy depths while Monica was straddling his face, rubbing her wetness all over him.

The two girls moaned and cried out as they both rode him and then he decided to take a more dominant role. He bucked them both off, causing them to complain, but he positioned them the way he wanted them and they were soon cooperating.

Rachel sat with her back against the headrail, her legs straight out. Clint laid Monica between Rachel's legs, the dark-haired girl's head in the blonde's lap, and then he straddled Monica and entered her. While fucking Monica that way he was able to lick and suck Rachel's breasts and kiss her mouth, fucking her with his tongue, sliding it in and out of her mouth. Abruptly, Rachel eased Monica's head down to the mattress so she could stand up with her feet on either side of her friend's head. That way Clint was able to lick her pussy while he continued to pound away at Monica, who was rubbing her hands up and down Rachel's legs. After a while they switched off, but then the girls had another idea, again.

Rachel got on her hands and knees and presented her round little bottom to Clint. He grasped her hips and entered her from behind, his penis still wet and slick enough to do this easily. Monica started out behind Clint, stroking his buttocks and back, imploring him to "fuck the little whore," and then she got her head down underneath them and was able to lick his balls, and the part of Clint's shaft that was not buried in Rachel.

And then once again they switched, and this time his penis was buried between Monica's ample ass cheeks while Rachel kissed him and stroked both of them. She slid one hand down between her friend's leg so she could touch Monica with one hand and Clint with the other. Suddenly, Monica was shuddering and crying out but Clint was not yet ready to go with her, so he allowed her to enjoy her passion alone, for now. When she was finished twitching and crying out he withdrew from her and moved over to enter Rachel in a more conventional manner. She was on her back and he grasped one of her ankles in each hand, spread her wide and plunged into her.

Monica reclined next to them, recovering from her own spasms, alternately stroking his bare buttocks or her friend's breasts. She pinched Rachel's nipples and then, while Clint continued to fuck her, leaned over to suck on her friend's breasts. The sight of the blonde Monica sucking on the dark-haired Rachel's nipples was more than Clint could take at that moment, and suddenly he was ejaculating, crying out as spasms so strong took hold of him that he was experiencing pleasure and pain at the same time . . .

"You girls are very close, aren't you?" he asked, later. He was lying on his back with a girl on either side of him.

"We are," Rachel said.

"We do everything together," Monica said.

"I can believe it," Clint said. He imagined that there was nothing these girls wouldn't do—and he wondered how much of it he could get them to show him in one night.

TWELVE

Clint woke the next morning tightly wedged between two naked women. It was certainly not the worst way a man could wake up. However, there was little chance of getting out of bed without waking them, and if he woke them he doubted he'd be able to make it out of bed.

When he finally decided to move, they moved, also. They rolled toward him, wedging him even tighter.

"Ladies," he said, "I do have to get up."

"Oh, don't worry," Monica said, "we're going to let you up. We're not ready for another go yet, honey."

"I'm tired," Rachel said. "You wore us both out."

It was true, he had to admit. Whether it was out of a desire to forget that his friend had been killed, or that he was simply *that* excited by having two beautiful women in bed with him, it had been he who woke them two more times during the night. They finally pleaded with him to let them sleep, and he finally fell asleep, as well.

But he woke with the first hint of light in the window, so now he eased from between them and was almost tempted to crawl back in when he saw them close the space he'd left and snuggle up to one another.

They were *very* close friends.

Clint was the first one at the graveyard, but was followed closely by Sheriff Champagne and then Peter Dexter. After that people started to drift in and, finally, the hearse made its way from town, bringing the body of Art Dwyer to its final resting place.

After a priest said a few words over the grave people began to move away, head back to town and back to their lives. Finally, there were only Dexter, the sheriff, and Clint left. Dexter then shook hands with both men and also left.

"He ain't gonna rest easy, you know," Tom Champagne said.

"I know."

"Not until we find Ramona."

"I know that."

Both men put on their hats and walked away from the grave and the graveyard. They walked back to town together and didn't stop until they had reached the livery. Without a word they each saddled their horse and walked them out of the barn. From there they went to the general store, where they picked up their supplies.

"Need anything from your hotel?" Champagne asked.

"Nope," Clint said. He didn't want the sheriff in his room, because he knew the two girls would still be there. Maybe the lawman wouldn't understand that he had needed some distraction last night. The two girls had understood it, but then that was the kind of thing women understood.

"Where do we start?" Champagne asked.

"The house," Clint said, "and the hill."

"Tracks around the house probably got trampled while people were trying to fight the fire."

"That's a good point," Clint said, "but we might be able to match some tracks near the house to those on the hill."

"Can you read sign that well?" Champagne asked. "Because I sure can't. I guess I've been sittin' around this town too long."

"Don't worry," Clint said. "I can read it."

"Then I guess we better get started."

They rode first to the hill, where Clint made note of the tracks there.

"This is odd."

"What is?" Champagne asked.

"There are six different tracks here, not five."

"That just means we're lookin' for one more man."

"No, but . . . there were two men on the hill, and there were three in town," Clint pointed out. "Who's the sixth man?"

"We'll find out the identity of the sixth man," Champagne said, "when we catch up to them."

"I suppose . . ." Clint said, but he was not appeased.

Next they rode down to the house. It took longer, because the ground around the house *had* been so badly trampled, but Clint was eventually able to pick up the trail.

"It gets clearer the farther away from the house we get," he explained.

"All six?"

"No," Clint said, shaking his head, "two, maybe three is all I can pick up."

"That's enough to follow."

"As long as they stay together," Clint said. "We don't want to have to split up."

"If we do," Champagne said, "you better find me some pretty easy sign to follow."

The trail led west, and as they got further from the house Clint was once again able to see all five tracks.

"If they've got Ramona with them," he said, "she must be riding double, at this point."

"Maybe they'll stop along the way to get her a horse."

"That would make sense."

They rode for half a day, passed a couple of towns, and still the men had made no attempt to obtain another horse.

"Still riding double," Clint said.

"I hear an 'or' in there, somewhere," Tom Champagne said.

"Or maybe she's not with them."

"If she's not with them," the sheriff said, "then where is she?"

"I don't know."

"You think she wandered off on her own," the lawman asked, "maybe lost her memory."

"If she did," Clint said, "her footprints were lost. We're just going to have to assume that she's still with them, until we find out something that tells us different."

"So we go on," Champagne said.

"We go on," Clint replied.

THIRTEEN

They camped that night and divided up the jobs. Champagne took care of the horses while Clint built the fire and started the coffee going.

"I have a question," Champagne said, as he sat across the fire from Clint and accepted a cup of coffee.

"Ask it."

"Is this seeming a little too easy for you?"

"How do you mean?"

"I mean we've got five sets of tracks, all staying together, making it fairly simply to follow them. Why don't they split up?"

"I'm expecting them to."

"But didn't you expect them to before now?" the lawman asked.

"Actually, yes."

"But they haven't," Champagne said. "Why not?"

"Maybe because they want us to catch up to them?"

"And why would they want that?" the sheriff asked. "To trap us? Why? What did we do except lose a friend?"

"Well, if they know that we were friends of Art's, and they expect us to track them, then they probably also know that we won't stop until we find them."

"So they're gonna let us find them, figuring they can outnumber us. That's why they're stayin' together."

"Of course," Clint said, "this theory goes to hell if we find that they've split up a little further up the trail."

"And what about the sixth man?" Champagne asked. "I've been thinking about him."

"So have I. Who is he, and why isn't he with them?"

"Could be he's somebody they're workin' for."

"Like Pete Dexter."

"You gonna start that again?" Champagne asked. "There are other ranchers living near Art Dwyer, Clint."

"Others who would benefit from his death?"

"Maybe."

"How?"

"Who says for sure that Dexter would get the army contract?" Tom Champagne asked.

"Pete Dexter said so."

"Well, he could be wrong," the sheriff said. "Maybe somebody else wanted a chance at it."

"Okay," Clint said, "so you come up with another name for the sixth man."

"I think I'll just wait until we catch up to the five, and let them tell us the name of the sixth."

"You have no problem taking on five men, just us two?"

"No problem at all."

"Why's that?"

" 'Cause of who you are," Champagne said. "I figure you'll take out four of them and I'll only have to handle one."

Clint stared at him and asked, "Beans or bacon?"
Champagne smiled and said, "I like both."

After Clint cooked up dinner—beans *and* bacon, and another pot of the trail coffee he'd been missing—they decided that Champagne would take the first four-hour watch.

"That'll get us up around six," Clint said. "I'll have a fresh pot of coffee ready and we can hit the trail early."

"Six," Champagne said. "Now I remember why I stopped riding the trail. Bein' a town sheriff you get to sleep real late—like till eight."

"Well, we'll wrap this little manhunt up real quick so you can get back to your late hours, Sheriff," Clint said. "A little more coffee before I turn in?"

FOURTEEN

About a day in front of Clint and Tom Champagne were Hal Ricks and Ben Gunner, in a town called Concord. They had split from the other men, with the intention of joining up again, real soon. By the time Clint Adams and Sheriff Tom Champagne caught up they intended to be all together again.

But for now Ricks and Gunner were in the Concord saloon, drinking—Ricks much heavier than Gunner.

"Well," he said, "you got to admit he pays the bills."

"That don't give him the right to the woman."

Actually, Gunner thought that did give the man the right to the woman, but he decided not to mention that. He finished his beer, which was only his second to Ricks's sixth.

"Hal," he said, "maybe we should turn in. It's late and we want to get an early start in the mornin'."

"Why?" Ricks demanded. "Because he said so?"

"Well . . . yeah."

Ricks gave Gunner an angry look and said, "Well,

maybe he's your boss, but he ain't mine. I'm gettin' another beer."

Gunner got one, too, but he didn't get to finish it. Halfway through his seventh beer Hal Ricks slumped over, his forehead bouncing off the table. Gunner struggled with the bigger man's weight, but managed to get him out of the saloon, into their hotel, and into his room and bed before going to his own room and collapsing on his bed, exhausted.

Gunner woke to the sound of someone pounding on his door. He staggered off the bed and to the door before he realized he was still fully dressed, gunbelt and all.

"Wha—" he said as he opened the door.

"Let's move," Hal Ricks said, looking as fresh as could be.

"Wha—"

"We got to get going, Gunner," Ricks said. "We got to meet the others at Cannon Wells, remember."

"I remember, but last night—"

"Last night was last night," Ricks said. "Get yourself together, man, and meet me at the livery."

Ricks slammed the door and Gunner staggered back to the bed and sat on it. He didn't know how Ricks could drink so much and be so fresh the next morning. He'd never figure that out.

FIFTEEN

"I'm awake," Tom Champagne said before Clint could nudge him with his foot. "Your coffee did it."

"What's wrong with my coffee?" Clint asked.

"Nothing," Champagne said, "except you make it so strong just the smell could wake the dead."

"My coffee is perfect."

Champagne sat up, shrugging off his blanket, and said, "Instead of arguing, how about just handing me a cup?"

"It'll start the day off right," Clint said, handing a cup over.

Holding the cup in both hands Champagne said, "I haven't slept on the ground in so long everything hurts. I'm just hoping your coffee will kill me before I feel worse."

"It'll get your blood going," Clint said. "How about breakfast?"

"I couldn't eat."

"Good," Clint said, "then we can get started early.

You can saddle the horses while I kill the fire. It'll work the kinks out for you."

"I think this coffee has already killed the kinks," Champagne said, standing.

"Give it back, then, if it's so bad."

Clint reached but the sheriff pulled the cup out of his reach.

"I'll take it with me," Champagne said, getting to his feet with a groan, "it'll wake the horses."

"Shit!"

Ben Gunner dropped his horse's left foreleg to the ground and straightened up to face Hal Ricks.

"He stepped on something," he complained. "I need to find another horse. This one is lame."

"I can't wait," Ricks said. "I'll go on and meet the others while you get yourself a new mount and follow."

Gunner looked around helplessly.

"We're in the middle of nowhere."

"There's a town a few miles east of here called Willoughby," Ricks said. "This horse should get you that far."

"Then what am I supposed to do?" Gunner demanded. "Buy a horse?"

"Buy one, steal one, I don't care," Ricks said, "just meet us at Cannon Wells."

"Fine, fine," Gunner said, "go on, you go ahead. I'll be along as soon as I can."

Ricks mounted his horse and looked down at the agitated Gunner.

"Don't take too long, Ben," he said. "You want to be there for the big finish, don't ya?"

"Yeah, yeah," Gunner said, "the big finish, five men gunnin' down one old gunfighter."

"I wouldn't call Clint Adams an 'old' gunfighter," Ricks said.

"Well, he ain't young," Gunner groused.

"Better get movin', Gunner," Ricks said. "Don't fall more than a day behind."

"Right, right," Gunner said, waving Ricks away.

"Remember," Ricks said, turning his horse. "No more than a day."

Gunner watched Ricks ride off, then turned and glared at his horse.

"I ain't walkin' a few miles," he told the animal. "I'll ride you into the ground first."

He mounted the horse and rode it east, trying to ignore the fact that the animal was limping.

"Okay," Clint said, staring at the ground.

"What?"

Clint dismounted and studied the ground.

"This is where they split." He stood up and pointed. "Two that way, three that way."

"Two continuing on the way we're going?" Champagne said. "Why are the other three going that way?"

Clint stood up and stared at the lawman.

"They trying to split us up."

"But we're not gonna bite, right?"

"Right."

Clint mounted up again.

"We'll stay on the trail of the two and let the three think they're baiting us," Clint explained.

"Maybe we'll catch up to the two before they join back with the other three," Champagne said. "That way splittin' up will hurt them, not us."

"Good thinking, Sheriff," Clint said. "Let's hope it goes that way."

"Sure," Tom Champagne said, "then we'll only have to take one each to start."

"Maybe," Clint said, "I should make you show me how well you handle a gun before we go any further."

"Naw," Champagne said, "I think I'll just let it be a surprise."

SIXTEEN

Willoughby was a small town where a stranger probably stood out when he rode in. For this reason Ben Gunner dismounted and walked the limping horse in. He felt this way even if he was noticed it would be fairly obvious why he was there, and there wouldn't be so much curiosity about him.

He found his way to the livery and was met out front by an older man wiping his hands on a grimy rag and chewing a huge wad of tobacco.

"Problem with your horse?" the man asked.

Smart man, Gunner thought sarcastically, but kept it to himself.

"Stupid animal stepped on something," Gunner said. "Do you have any horses for sale?"

"Nope," the man said, spitting out a wad of tobacco juice. "May not need a new one, though. Lemme take a look at him."

"I don't have time to wait for him to heal," Gunner said. "I need a new horse."

"Ain't got none," the man said. "Small town, ya

know? Lemme have a look at him for ya."

Gunner handed the reins over to the old man and said, "Okay, have a look, then."

The old man took the horse and walked it into the livery, yelling over his shoulder, "Get yerself a drink while yer waitin'."

That, at least, sounded like good advice.

"This is odd," Clint said, later in the day.

"What is?"

"Well," he said, "these two have split up, now."

"What? Why'd they do that? Tryin' to split us up, again, if we didn't go for it the first time?"

Clint dismounted and studied the ground for a while.

"I can read sign," Clint said, "but I'm no expert—"

"But?"

"But it looks to me like this one's mount is favoring his right foreleg," Clint said.

He stood up and stared east.

"Is there a town that way?"

"A small one called Willoughby."

"Well, maybe we caught a break, Sheriff," Clint said. "Maybe one of their horses stepped on something, or in something, and he's on his way to Willoughby to find a new one."

"Willoughby's pretty small," Champagne said. "Might not be any horses there to buy."

"Any law there?"

"No, why?"

"Might not be any horses there to buy," Clint said, mounting up, "but maybe a few to steal."

SEVENTEEN

Clint and Sheriff Tom Champagne rode into Willoughby after dark and proceeded directly to the livery stable. The doors were not locked and they walked their mounts in and looked around.

"Here," Clint said, "there's a horse in this stall."

They found a lamp and lit it, then Champagne held both horses while Clint moved into the stall to check out the other horse.

"Looks like a stone bruise, left forefront," he called out.

"There are no other horses in here," Champagne said. "Maybe the owner is still in town."

"Do you know who the liveryman is here?"

"Last time I was here it was an old-timer named Leon." Champagne looked around on the ground for a few moments, then said, "Yeah, it's still Leon."

"How can you tell?" Clint asked.

"All these dark patches on the ground are tobacco juice," Champagne said. "Leon goes to sleep with a plug and gets up in the morning with one."

61

"Okay," Clint said, "so let's find Leon."

"He sleeps in a shack at the north end of town."

"Let's take our horses, in case the owner of this one comes back."

Champagne agreed, and they walked with their horses to Leon's run-down shack at the end of town. They tied their horses off and approached the shack. From inside came a terrible racket and it took a few moments before they realized it was the sound of a man snoring.

They entered and Champagne found a lamp. Once they lit it they saw the old man sleeping on a pallet against the wall. He was lying on his back and every time he snored, a brown bubble of tobacco juice would appear on his lips.

"Jesus," Clint said, disgusted.

"I'll wake him."

Clint wondered how the man didn't drown to death.

Champagne shook the man said, "Come on, Leon, wake up."

The old man came awake and spit a projectile of tobacco juice across the room. It just missed Champagne at the point of take off and then missed Clint as it landed on the wall behind him. He turned and watched it drip down the wall.

"Jesus," he said again.

"Leon, are you awake?" Champagne asked.

Leon made a terrible noise as he cleared his throat and Clint readied himself for another wad of tobacco juice, which thankfully didn't come.

"What?" Leon said. "Who is it?"

"It's Sheriff Champagne, Leon," the lawman said, "from Two Forks. You remember me?"

"Yeah, yeah, I remember," Leon said. "Tom Champagne."

"That's right."

"What the hell'r you doin' wakin' me up?" Leon complained.

"I've got to ask you some questions, Leon."

Leon looked past Champagne at Clint.

"Who's that feller?"

"His name is Clint Adams."

"The Gunsmith?"

"That's right."

Leon looked at Clint.

"What the hell'r you doin' in a shithole like this?"

"Asking you some questions, Leon," Clint said.

"Well then, ask," Leon said, "and lemme get back ta sleep."

"There's a horse in your stable," Champagne said.

"Yep, finally got me some business."

"Who brought it in?"

"Some feller," Leon said. "He was lookin' ta buy a new horse."

"And what did you tell him?"

"First I tol' him I didn't have none to sell," Leon explained, "and then I tol' him ta lemme look at his, maybe he didn't need no new horse."

"And does he?"

"Not if he waits long enough for this one to heal," the old man said, "only he ain't too keen on waitin'. Says he's got to meet somebody someplace."

"So can you get him another horse?"

"Nope."

"Maybe he'll steal one."

The old man cackled at that, then started to choke. Clint danced one way and then the other, getting ready to dodge a gob of tobacco juice. When it came it just missed him and he gave a sigh of relief.

"What's so funny?" he asked.

"There ain't even a horse in this town ta steal."

"So then he's still here?"

"Yup."

"Where?" the sheriff asked.

"Last I saw he was in the saloon," Leon said. "That's where he was when I give him the news."

Champagne looked at Clint, who nodded because he wanted to get out of there.

"Okay, Leon," Champagne said, "go back to sleep."

"Thanks, Sheriff," Leon said, and flopped into his back. He was snoring and bubbling again before they got out of the room.

Outside Champagne said, "Good thing Leon was too deeply asleep, we would have gotten nothing out of him."

"He wasn't deeply asleep?"

"Sometimes that old man sleeps like the dead."

"I'm just glad he can't hit a moving target," Clint said.

EIGHTEEN

They went back to the livery and left their horses there, still saddled because they didn't know what the rest of the night would bring. They also left their rifles behind, figuring handguns would be good enough in the saloon.

"Want me to come in the back?" Champagne asked.

"Why don't we both just walk in the front and see what happens?" Clint asked. "I mean, how big is this saloon?"

"It's the biggest building in town," Champagne said. "When this town was first built some folks had high hopes for it. They built the saloon in anticipation of that."

"And what happened?"

Champagne looked at him.

"Nothing," he said, "that was the problem."

They continued on to the saloon and Clint saw what the sheriff had meant. The saloon was big enough to be smack dab in the middle of Dodge City, but here it was, in Willoughby.

They mounted the boardwalk and peered in the window. There were two people inside, the bartender and one man sitting at a table, slumped over a drink, looking miserable.

"Must be our man," Clint said.

"He don't look too happy."

"What do you say we make him even less happy?"

They entered through the batwing doors.

After Leon had delivered the bad news to Ben Gunner the outlaw had sought comfort from a bottle of whiskey. He was stuck in Willoughby either until his horse healed or until a horse appeared that he could steal.

What the hell kind of town doesn't even have a horse to steal?

He was on his second bottle of watered-down whiskey when the two men walked through the batwing doors of the saloon and approached the bar. Gunner knew the whiskey was watered down because he was usually unconscious before he finished one whole bottle, and here he was halfway through a second.

He'd been in the saloon for hours and in all that time not one other soul had walked in. He had invited the bartender to drink with him, but the man had insisted he didn't drink. Now, suddenly, two new friends had appeared.

"Barkeep!" he shouted. "Whatever my two new friends are having put it on my tab." After all, he had all that money, his share of what he and Ricks and the others had been paid to kill that rancher and burn him out.

"Much obliged, friend," Clint called back. "We'll have a couple of beers and drink to your generosity."

"Well, then you bring them beers over here, stranger, and drink 'em with me."

"We'll do that."

Clint turned to Champagne and said something, and the lawman removed his badge and put it in his pocket. They then picked up their beers and walked over to join their host.

"My name's Ben Gunner," the outlaw said, "and I'm buyin' as long as you're drinkin'."

"That's real friendly, Ben," Clint said. "I'm Clint and this is Tom."

"Pleased ta meet both of you."

They each sipped their beer and then Clint said, "You mind us asking why you're being so generous?"

"That's a good question," Gunner said, peering at them with one eye closed. "See, I'm stuck in this rathole of a town—" Suddenly, Gunner clasped his hand over his mouth, then looked around before continuing. "Sorry, You don't live here, do ya?"

"No," Clint said, also keeping his voice low, "we think it's a rathole, too."

"Good." Gunner started to laugh and they had to wait until he got tired, or had to take a breath.

"How'd you get stuck here?"

"My horse went lame," Gunner said, "and they ain't got another one in this town. Can you believe that?"

"Sure can," Clint said. "After all, it's a rathole, right?"

That started Gunner laughing all over again, until he almost choked. Clint was glad the man wasn't chewing tobacco.

"You on your way somewhere?" Clint asked.

"I'm supposed to be meeting some friends."

"Oh? Where?"

"Place called Cannon Wells. Ever hear of it?"

"I haven't," Clint said, "but maybe my friend has.

He's from around here. You ever hear of Cannon Wells, Sheriff?"

"Sure," Champagne said. "It's about a day's ride from here."

"All your friends meeting you there?" Clint asked.

"Yup," Gunner said, "four of 'em. We done a job together, and now—" Abruptly, Gunner stopped as something registered. Something somebody had just said.

"W-wait a minute . . ." he said, frowning.

"What's wrong?" Clint asked.

He looked at Champagne, who had slipped his badge out of his pocket and was pinning it back onto his shirt.

Gunner saw the badge and peered at it.

"Did—did you c-call him sheriff?"

"I did."

"How come?"

"Well, because that's what he is," Clint said. "He's the sheriff of a town called Two Forks."

"Tw-Two—Two Forks?"

"That's right."

Gunner peered at him.

"And who're you?"

"My name's Clint Adams."

"Adams?"

"That's right."

"The, uh, Gunsmith Adams? That Adams?"

"That's right," Clint said. "I'm the guy who was a friend of Art Dwyer's. You remember Art Dwyer, don't you?"

"D-Dwyer?"

"The man you killed?" Clint asked. "You and your friends? You beat him, and shot him and burned his place down. Remember? That little job you did together?"

"Hey," Gunner said, "hey, wait a minute—hey—y-you ain't no new friends of mine."

"I'll bet," Clint said, "you've never said truer words in your life, Gunner."

NINETEEN

Clint and Champagne spent the night in the Willoughby hotel, to the delight of the owner, who had not had a guest in weeks.

"We'll need two rooms," Champagne told the man, showing him his badge. "We'll be keeping a prisoner in one of them."

The man's heart sank when he saw the badge. He knew he'd never see the money for the two rooms from the county.

Clint and the sheriff took turns watching over Ben Gunner all night. The man was so drunk he slept most of the night, but they knew he could wake at any time and try to escape. They wanted to question him again in the morning, when he was sober.

Clint was with him, sitting in a chair by the window as first light streamed in and woke the man.

"What the—who are you?" Gunner demanded. "Where the hell am I?"

"I'm Clint Adams," Clint said. "We met last night.

You bought me a drink. You're in a hotel in a town called Willoughby."

"Jesus," Gunner said, "I'm still in Willoughby?"

"That's right."

"That damned horse!" Gunner swore. He started to get up and Clint said, "Don't."

"What?"

"Don't get up."

"Why not? And what are you doin' in my room?"

"You're a prisoner, Ben," Clint said. "Sheriff Tom Champagne of Two Forks is in the room next door. He'll be coming in here shortly."

"What are you talkin ab—where's my gun?"

"We took it away from you."

"You took it—what the hell . . . was I drunk last night?"

"As a skunk."

"So you took advantage of me?"

"We arrested you, you sorry shit," Clint said.

Gunner sank back down on the bed as this information began to sink in.

"I'm under arrest?"

"That's right."

"For what?"

"For killing Art Dwyer and burning his place to the ground."

A crafty look came onto the man's face.

"Did I say I done that?"

"No," Clint said, "you said you and your friends had done it, and they were waiting for you in Cannon Wells."

Gunner covered his face with his hands and made a disgusted sound.

"Jesus Christ, I'm gonna get killed!" he said.

"By who?"

"By . . . wait a minute, never mind, by who," the man shouted. "I ain't tellin' you nothin'."

"You've already told us enough, Ben," Clint said. "Why not just tell it all."

"All?"

"You fellas didn't just decide to kill Art Dwyer and burn him out," Clint said, "you were hired to do it."

"Hired."

"That's right," Clint said. "You just have to tell us by who?"

Gunner thought a moment, then said, "I can't tell you that."

"Why not?"

"It would get me killed."

"Not if we arrest all your partners, and the man who hired you," Clint said. "Who's going to kill you then?"

"You think I'd be safe in prison?" Gunner asked. "They could get to me easy in prison."

"Well, what if you never make it to prison?"

"What? You'd let me go?"

"Or kill you myself," Clint said. "One or the other."

Gunner squinted at Clint.

"Which one?"

"I don't know," Clint said. "I haven't made up my mind about that yet."

Just then there was a knock on the door.

"Come on in," Clint said.

The door opened and Sheriff Tom Champagne walked in.

"So, he's awake?"

"He's awake."

"Talkin'?"

"Not much."

"Why not?"

"Seems he's afraid he's going to get killed if he talks."

"You explain to him he might get killed if he don't talk?"

"I was trying to make that clear when you got here."

"He—he said you could k-kill me, or let me go," Gunner blurted.

"You told him that?" Champagne asked.

"I might have."

The lawman looked at the prisoner.

"He can kill you, Gunner, but he can't let you go."

"Why not?"

"Well, because he's not the sheriff," Champagne said, "I am."

"Then you can let me go."

"Or," Champagne said, "I can let him kill you."

"Well . . . which one is it?" Gunner asked.

Champagne rubbed his chin and then said, "I don't know. I haven't decided yet."

TWENTY

There was one place in Willoughby to get breakfast, a small cafe Tom Champagne remembered.

"If it's still there," he said.

It was. They told Ben Gunner that they would buy him breakfast while they decided whether to kill him or let him go.

The food at the cafe wasn't very good and the coffee was weak, but then how much practice did they get actually cooking for strangers? Anyway, the food wasn't important. What was more important was the act they were putting on for the benefit of the prisoner.

"I say he's not going to talk," Clint said, "we just kill him."

"Now, wait a minute," Champagne said. "He hasn't said he won't talk. If he does, we can just let him go."

"Why should we let him go?" Clint asked. "He's already told us his friends will be at Cannon Wells. All we have to do is go there and get them."

"But maybe there's more he can tell us," Champagne said.

"Like what?"

Champagne leaned forward and said in a low voice, "The name of the man who hired them."

"Ah," Clint said, "the sixth man."

Gunner was watching them, sitting between them and turned his head this way and that when each spoke.

"You know," Clint said, "that's about the only thing that'll keep me from killing him. The name of the man who hired them."

Both men turned their heads and looked at Gunner.

"I don't know," the outlaw said. "I swear, I don't know. It was Ricks who was hired—" He stopped short, then realized it was too late. He'd already spoken the name.

"Ricks?" Clint asked.

"Hal Ricks?" Champagne said. "That's who you're ridin' with? That's who killed Art Dwyer?"

"You know him?" Clint asked.

"Hell, yeah, I know him," Champagne said. "There ain't a more worthless piece of trash on earth."

"Did he know Dwyer?"

"Not that I know of."

"What about it, Gunner?" Clint asked. "Did Ricks know Dwyer?"

"No . . . but he knew Dwyer's wife."

"What?" Champagne asked. "That lowlife knew Ramona?"

"Her name wasn't Ramona, when he knew her," Gunner said.

"What was it?" Clint asked.

"He never said," Gunner replied. "All he said was that he knew her before."

"How well?"

"Real well, according to him."

"That can't be," Champagne said. He looked at Clint. "You met Ramona. She wouldn't have anything to do with the likes of Hal Ricks."

"I only just met her, Tom," Clint said. "I didn't know anything about her. Hell, Art was my friend, but I didn't know what she was doing with him—and neither did he."

Champagne opened his mouth to protest, but he couldn't. Clint was speaking the truth.

"Who knows who she was or who she was with before she met Art?" Clint asked.

"Gunner, Ricks is gonna be at Cannon Wells?" Champagne asked.

"Yeah."

"With who?"

"Three guys he hired," Gunner said. "I don't even remember all their names."

"Try," Champagne said.

"One was Clell Miller," Gunner said. "I don't know the others."

"One got a scar?" Clint asked. "Here?"

"Yeah, that's right."

"One talk about his daddy when you call him a pig?" Champagne asked.

"That's Miller," Gunner said, shaking his head. "He loves tellin' you he takes after his daddy. How do you know all this?"

"We got descriptions of those three," Champagne said. "It's you and Ricks we didn't know about."

"But now we do," Clint said.

"So whataya gonna do with me, huh?" Gunner said. "Kill me or let me go. I tol' ya what I know."

"Well," Champagne said, "I can't very well let you go, Gunner. I'm a peace officer."

Gunner's eyes went wide.

"You're gonna let him kill me?"

"Now, take it easy," Champagne said, "I can't do that, either."

"Then what?"

"Well . . . we'll have to lock you up someplace until we get back," Champagne said. "You and Ricks and the others will have to pay for killing Dwyer and his men."

"That was Ricks. He did it."

"He killed all six?" Clint asked.

"He killed Dwyer," Gunner said. "That got the others started shootin', and by the time it was over, everybody was dead."

"Not everybody, Gunner," Clint said.

"Whataya mean?"

"The woman," Clint said. "Dwyer's wife, whatever her real name was. What happened to her?"

"Does Ricks have her?" Champagne asked.

"Naw, Ricks ain't got 'er," Gunner said. "He was real upset about that. He wanted her."

"So what happened?"

"The feller that hired us," Gunner said, "He wanted her, too."

"And he got her?" Clint asked.

"I guess," Gunner said.

"What do you mean, you guess?" Champagne asked. "He either got her or he didn't."

"All I know is that Ricks ain't got 'er," Gunner said. "I don't know who does, 'cause I don't know who hired us. Only Ricks knew that."

"And Ricks and the others are waitin' for us at Cannon Wells?" Champagne asked.

"That's right."

"And they're waiting there for you, too, aren't they, Gunner?" Clint asked slowly.

"That's right."

"Tom," Clint said, "I'm thinking maybe we don't have to leave Mr. Gunner here, locked up someplace."

"You getting' an idea?" Champagne asked.

Clint nodded and said, "Yep, I'm getting an idea."

TWENTY-ONE

When he thought about it for a while Ben Gunner decided he would rather have been left behind, locked up somewhere. Being taken along with Clint Adams and Sheriff Tom Champagne to Cannon Wells, there was a real good chance he would end up dead.

It was a full day's ride to Cannon Wells, so they knew they'd be camping somewhere close by come nightfall, and then planned to ride in the next morning. They rode with Gunner between them, his hands tied to the saddlehorn, the reins of his horse in Sheriff Tom Champagne's hands.

"Tell me about Cannon Wells," Clint said. "What kind of town is it?"

"It's not a town," Champagne said. "It's an old stagecoach way station, abandoned now. It's almost a fortress, though, surrounded by a stone wall. It'd be hell getting somebody out of there if they were dug in real good."

"Guess we'll have to figure out some way to get in, instead of a way to get them out."

"Oh, I'm sure Gunner, here," Champagne said, slapping the man on the back heartily, "will be happy to help us with that."

"You're jest getting me killed," Gunner said, shaking his head, "that's all. Ya shoulda shot me yourself back in town."

"Look on the bright side, Gunner," Champagne said. "If not for us, old Leon would still have you convinced your horse wasn't ready to travel, and you'd still be paying him to board it."

"If that old man hadn't lied to me I woulda been long gone before you even got there," Gunner grumbled.

"That's the breaks, Gunner," Champagne said, "that's the breaks."

In Cannon Wells, Clell Miller asked Hal Ricks, "How long we gonna wait for Gunner?"

"I told you, we ain't waitin' for Gunner," Ricks said, "we're waitin' for Adams."

"That's just suicide," Miller complained. "Why we got to wait on a man like the Gunsmith?"

"Because we're gettin' paid to."

"Why we got to kill him, anyway?"

"Because he was friends with Art Dwyer, and he won't stop looking until he finds the men who killed his friend," Ricks explained. "That means you, me, and the others, Miller. You got that? It's kill him or he'll hunt us down one by one. That's why we have to stick together."

"Okay!" Miller said. "You know, this'd be a lot easier ta take if we'd brought the woman here with us. Coulda passed her around, ya know?"

"Clell, you're a pig," Ricks said.

Clell Miller grinned and said, "Jest like my daddy."

TWENTY-TWO

They camped for the night and left Gunner tied to a tree. Actually, they tied his legs to a tree but left his hands free so he could eat.

"This is embarrassin'," Gunner said.

"More embarrassing than hanging?" Clint asked.

That quieted him down and he ate the plate of bacon and beans Clint handed him.

Clint went back to the fire and picked up his own plate. Champagne was half done with his, already.

"So how do we play this?" the lawman asked.

"Well, we brought Gunner along, so we might as well use him to get us in," Clint replied.

"How?"

"He can say he ran into us along the way and recruited us to help with you and me."

"Huh?"

"He recruited us—two more outlaws—to help with the sheriff and the Gunsmith."

"Oh. Think they'll buy that?"

"I don't know," Clint said. "I'm open to a suggestion if you have a better idea."

"I don't," Champagne said, "right now."

"All right, then."

They set the watches again for the night, same order, Champagne first, and then Clint. This time they had to watch Ben Gunner, as well. It had been Clint's experience that a man who was tied up and wanted to get untied badly enough would find a way.

He slept well, but heard Champagne as he approached his bedroll to wake him.

"You sleep light," the lawman said.

"I stay alive that way."

They changed places, Champagne rolling himself up in his blanket.

"Is Gunner asleep?" Clint asked.

"He hasn't been," Champagne said. "I think he's a little worried about tomorrow."

"Can't blame him for that," Clint said. "Coffee?"

"You hate my coffee," Champagne reminded him, rolling over. "Make it yourself."

Clint couldn't argue with that, so he made a pot and then offered a cup to Gunner.

"Sure, why not?" the outlaw answered. "I can't sleep, anyway."

Clint carried the cup over to Gunner.

"Can you untie my legs?" Gunner asked. "My knees hurt. I wanna stretch 'em."

"Sure," Clint said, "but if you run I'll really make your knees hurt—by putting a bullet in each one. Understand?"

"I understand."

Clint untied him and Gunner grunted as he got to his feet. He walked in circles, drinking the coffee.

"God, this is strong," he said.

"Then don't drink it."

"Naw, it's okay."

Clint sat and drank his, keeping a watchful eye on Gunner.

"Tell me somethin'."

"What?"

"What are you gonna do when we get to Cannon Wells?"

"We're going to take Ricks and the others in."

"And then what?"

"Find out who hired Dwyer killed."

"And then are you gonna kill him?"

"I guess that'll be up to him."

"You wouldn'ta really killed me if I didn't talk to ya, would ya?"

"Guess you'll never know."

"I didn't pull no trigger, ya know."

"That right?"

"I just lit the house and barn afire . . . and I was told ta do that."

"And that makes it okay?"

"Don't it?"

"Sit back down," Clint said. "I've decided it's not a bad thing for your knees to hurt."

TWENTY-THREE

Clint watched Ben Gunner until the man finally fell asleep, his head back against the tree he was tied to. He didn't much care if the man got any sleep, but once he *was* asleep, it took some of the pressure off him.

He missed Duke when he was camped like this. The big black gelding was an early warning system, always sensing when someone or something was approaching the camp. Tom Champagne's horse and the steeldust just stood there like, well . . . horses.

Clint poured himself another cup of coffee and thought about Art Dwyer and his wife, Ramona. He wondered if it was true that this fella Ricks knew Ramona before, or if Ricks was just bragging to his friends that he'd known a beautiful woman before? And was that how Ramona had escaped the fate that had befallen Dwyer and his men? Because she had known Ricks before? And if that was the case, wouldn't she be with Ricks, instead of with this mysterious employer—this sixth man?

Clint drank his coffee and listened intently to what

was going on outside the circle of their camp—nothing.
It was quiet. He looked up. The moon was bright—so
bright they probably could have traveled. Maybe they
should have—maybe they should have sneaked into
Cannon Wells at night and gotten the drop on Ricks and
his men.

No, that would have been a bad idea. They were sure
to have a watch set, just the way Clint and Champagne
had. It was better to ride up in the morning, bold as
brass, with Ben Gunner leading them, and volunteer to
join them. Maybe Ricks would figure that seven against
two was much better odds than five against two. Once
they were inside and sort of trusted, then they could get
the drop on the others—if Ben Gunner went along with
them and didn't give them up.

Hal Ricks couldn't sleep. He was thinking about Ramona Dwyer—only, when he'd known her, she had
been a San Francisco whore named Maisie O'Donnell.
It had been pure coincidence that Ricks had gone to
check Dwyer out and had seen Maisie/Ramona with him
on his porch. He only had to ask his employer, Pete
Dexter, the story to find out that "Ramona" had come
to town looking for a job in the dress shop, had met
Dwyer, and had eventually married him. Once Ricks told
Dexter who Ramona really was the rancher had had a
big laugh on his competition, Art Dwyer.

"If I was going to leave him alive," Dexter had said,
"I'd tell him that his wife is really a whore."

But Dexter hadn't told Dwyer, and Ricks found out
why. The rancher wanted Ramona for himself. Finding
out she'd been a whore had only seemed to make him
more interested.

Well, Ricks hadn't minded killing Dwyer and burning

his place. He hadn't even minded killing Dwyer's men, but he had minded handing Ramona over to Dexter. That was something he was going to remedy as soon as he and his men finished with Clint Adams and that sheriff from Two Forks.

He walked to the window of the abandoned station building and stared out into the darkness. Where the hell was Gunner? He should have been back by now. Four against two didn't sound like the greatest of odds to him, not when one of the two was the Gunsmith. He'd been counting on his five man to two advantage.

Clell Miller, who was on watch, came walking past the window, disproving Ricks' belief that the man was out there someplace, asleep.

"What are you doin' up, Ricks?" Miller asked.

"Can't sleep."

"Well, hell, I could," Miller said, "but I got an hour to go on my watch."

"Who's spellin' you?"

"Browning."

"Come on in and get some sleep," Ricks said. "I'll wake Browning in an hour."

"Hey, thanks!" Miller said.

"No problem," Ricks said. "Hell, I can't sleep, anyway. Maybe I'll just let all of you sleep til mornin'."

Miller met Ricks at the door and passed him his rifle.

"See ya in the mornin'," he said, and tumbled into a bunk. Ricks went outside and closed the door behind him.

By morning Clint had a fresh pot of coffee going. The smell of it woke both Champagne and Gunner. He handed each of them a cup before pouring one for himself.

"Dream up any better plans while you were asleep?" Clint asked the sheriff.

Champagne rubbed his face with both hands then picked his cup up from the ground.

"If I had any dreams, I can't remember them."

"Well then, I guess we'll stick with the one we've got."

"I've got a plan," Ben Gunner said.

Both men looked at the outlaw.

"Let's turn around and go back," Gunner said. "I'm not lookin' forward to gettin' killed."

"Gunner," Clint said, "you've only got one way to get out of this alive."

"And what's that?"

"Go along with us," Clint said. "When we get to Cannon Wells if you give us away, I'll make sure you get the first bullet. Do you understand?"

"I understand," Gunner said. "I can get killed by you, or by Ricks."

"Or you can stay alive by helping us," Clint said. "I won't let Ricks kill you."

"And will you keep me from gettin' hung?"

Clint looked at Champagne.

"That's up to a jury, Gunner," the lawman said. "You tell them your story and see what happens."

Gunner shook his head and said, "This ain't gonna come out good."

"You got that right, Gunner," Clint said. "It can't come out good, but it might come out better than you think."

TWENTY-FOUR

"There it is," Champagne said.

"Oh, God," Gunner said.

"It does look like a fortress," Clint said.

"Jesus," Gunner said, "I'm gonna puke."

"Do it now, Gunner," Clint said, "because if you do it down there, it will be the last thing you ever do."

"Christ," Gunner said, but he didn't puke.

"Let's go," Clint said. "Tom?"

"Yeah?"

"I'd put that badge someplace else if I was you."

"Oh . . . right . . ."

"Ricks?"

Hal Ricks came out of the station house when he heard Clell Miller call his name.

"What is it?"

"We got company."

"Who?"

"It's Gunner."

"It's about time."

"And he's bringin' company with him."

"Who?"

"Two men," Miller said. "Don't know who they are."

"Browning? Sinclair?"

The two men came running out.

"Get into position," Ricks said. "We don't know what we have here."

"Right," Browning said.

"Okay," Sinclair said.

Ricks moved up to the wall, next to Clell Miller, so he could see who was coming.

"Recognize 'em?" Miller asked.

"Not from here," Ricks said. "They'll have to get a little closer before I can tell."

"When they're close enough to kill," Miller said, "you just say the word."

"I just thought of something," Clint said, as they rode closer to the station.

"What?" Champagne asked.

"Well, three of these men were in Two Forks."

"Right."

"In the saloon."

"Right again."

"And you went into the saloon to take a look at them."

"Right."

"Did you talk to them?"

"Nope," Champagne said, "just took a look."

"And do you think they took a look at you?"

Champagne hesitated, then said, "Well, Jesus, I hope not."

Clint didn't reply.

Gunner said, "Jesus Christ."

"That's how I feel about it," Champagne said. "That's a helluva thing to bring up now, ain't it?"

"Well," Clint said, with a shrug, "it just . . . sort of . . . occurred to me."

"It couldn't have occurred to you sooner?" Champagne asked.

Clint didn't really think he wanted an answer.

TWENTY-FIVE

"Hold it right there!" Hal Ricks called out.

Ben Gunner froze. On either side of him Clint and Champagne were ready for anything. If Gunner gave them away they'd have to get their guns out fast, as there were already four guns trained on them.

The tense moment lengthened until Ricks finally spoke again.

"Who are your friends, Ben?" he asked. "And why are they with you?"

Clint and Champagne had fed Ricks phony names and a phony story. Now they waited to see what was going to come out of his mouth.

"They wanna join up, Hal," Gunner finally called out. "Ran into them in Willoughby while I was waitin' for my horse to be worked on."

"That's the same horse, ain't it?" Ricks asked.

"Yeah, it is," Gunner said, "turns out he wasn't as lame as I thought. Just needed to stay off his foot for a day."

Ricks was studying Clint and Champagne very

closely. Clint wondered if the man had seen the sheriff at all, if he had even been in Two Forks before the attack on Dwyer. As for himself—well, Ricks could have seen him anywhere over the years. Maybe this outlaw was the type who stuck to his own bailiwick.

"What are yer names?" Ricks asked.

Clint was glad of this, because he'd been worried that Gunner might forget the names they had given him.

"I'm Carl Allen," Clint said, "this here's my partner, Tim Carter."

"Where are you from?"

"Around," Champagne said.

"Here and there," Clint said.

"Why do you want to join up with us?"

"We heard you were lookin' for some extra guns," Champagne said.

"You heard wrong," Ricks said. He looked at Gunner. "You tell them that Ben?"

"He didn't exactly tell us that," Clint said. "He told us you were gonna have a run in with the Gunsmith. We figured a couple extra guns wouldn't hurt you."

Ricks studied them, then said, "Well, you figured that right, but what do you think is in it for you?"

"Hey," Clint said, "we throw in with the bunch that killed the Gunsmith. You can get a lot of free meals out of a reputation like that."

"And women," Champagne said.

"I hear that," Clell Miller said, with a wide grin.

"You're a pig, Clell," Ricks said.

"Yep," Miller said, "jest like my daddy."

If there had been any doubt that they had the right bunch, that clinched it right there.

•   •   •

Ricks kept them waiting long enough for Gunner to really start sweating before he said, "Okay, Ben, bring your new friends in—but the rest of you keep an eye on them."

"You're careful," Clint said. "I like that."

"It's how I keep alive," Ricks said.

"I hear that."

"Come on in," Ricks said.

Clint, Gunner, and Champagne all rode into the midst of the outlaws together. If there was ever a time for Gunner to turn on them it was now, but the man kept silent.

"Sinclair, show them where to put their horses," Ricks said. "Ben, I want to talk to you inside."

Clint and Champagne gave each other a quick look. If Ricks took Gunner out of their sight, they were dead. The man was sure to spill his guts when he and Ricks were alone.

"Hey, Tim," Clint said, "take my horse, will ya. I want to get a look at the inside." He looked at Ricks. "Do you mind?"

Ricks stared at him, then said, "No, come on in. There's coffee on."

"Thanks."

Clint walked up next to his new friend, Gunner, and slapped him on the back.

"Looks like you were right about your buddy Ricks," he said. "He thinks of everything."

"Yeah," Gunner said, "everything."

TWENTY-SIX

The inside was bare except for a wooden table, some
chairs, and some bunks that were set against the walls.
Apparently, the gang had brought in some blankets for
the bunks. There was a wood burning stove against the
back wall and a pot of coffee on it.

"You mind?" Clint asked.

"Help yourself."

Clint walked over to the coffeepot, found a cup that
wasn't too dirty, used the tail of his shirt to clean it out,
and then filled it. That was when he heard the shot, and
then the second one. He controlled his reaction, turned,
and faced the two men. Ricks had his gun out, and Gunner was looking stunned.

"That was your friend, the sheriff, getting his," Ricks
said. "Did you really think you could ride in here like
that and take us? That easy?"

Clint had the coffee cup in his left hand.

"That was my friend the sheriff taking care of your
men," Clint said.

"Three of them?" Ricks asked. "With two shots?"

Clint smiled.

"The third man got smart and tossed his gun."

"I don't think so."

"Suit yourself." He sipped the coffee and made a face. "Man, you should be shot just for making this coffee."

"Look who's talkin'," Gunner said.

"You shouldn't have brought them in here, Gunner," Ricks said.

"They made me, Hal. They were gonna kill me."

"We'll talk about that later. You got your gun out?"

"Uh, no."

"Take it out and point it at him."

"Don't," Clint said.

"Do it, Ben."

"If you touch your gun, Ben," Clint said, "I'll have to kill you."

"Hey, cow pie," Ricks said to Clint. "In case you haven't noticed, I have a gun on you."

"It doesn't matter," Clint said. "I can draw and fire before you pull the trigger."

"Can't be done," Ricks said.

"It can."

"How do you know?"

"You should have shot me in the back," Clint said, "but you didn't. Do you know why?"

"Why?"

"Because you think you can take me," Clint said. "Oh, not fair and square, but you think that havin' your gun out gives you an edge. Well, it doesn't."

"You're bluffin'."

"Pull the trigger, then," Clint said. "Go ahead—but when you do, don't look at your gun."

"Wha—" Ricks said, and looked at his gun for just a split second. That was when Clint moved.

He drew and dropped, firing at the same time. The split second that Ricks had taken his eye off Clint cost the man his life. The bullet struck him in the belly and his eyes went wide with shock. He fired his gun into the floor as he fell forward onto his knees.

Gunner was shocked into action. He went for his gun, despite the fact that Clint yelled, "Don't." It was too late. Clint had no choice but to fire, and the bullet hit Gunner in the chest, knocking him over a chair and onto his back. He was dead before the back of his head bounced off the floor.

Clint started for the door but it opened and a man came stumbling in, followed by Champagne, who had his gun out.

"This is Clell Miller," Champagne said. The lawman looked around. "Looks like he's the last one left alive."

"I hope he knows more than Gunner knew," Clint said.

"That ain't hard," Miller said. "Gunner was an idiot."

"You ain't too smart, either," Champagne said. "He was sending signals to his partners that I could read loud and clear. I shot the two of them and this one never cleared leather. That makes him the smart one of the bunch."

Clint walked over to check on Ricks and Gunner, just to make sure they were dead.

"Okay," he said, ejecting the spent shells from his gun and loading in fresh ones, "what do we do with this one?"

"Take him back with us, I guess," Champagne said.

"You can't prove nothin'," Miller said.

"You were with them," Clint said, "and Gunner admitted that you all killed Dwyer and burned out his place. That's proof enough."

"Wait a minute," Miller said. "Maybe we can make a deal."

"There's only one thing you could possibly deal with," Clint said.

"What's that?"

"The name of the man who hired you."

"I—I can give you that."

"Liar," Champagne said. "Ricks is the only one who talked to him."

"But Ricks talked to me."

"Okay, then," Clint said, "who was it?"

"I'll tell you," Miller said, "when I'm safe and sound in Two Forks. I'm not gonna have you two kill me and leave my body here with them."

"We're takin' you all in," Champagne said, "them dead, and you . . . well, that's your choice."

"I can't talk if I'm dead," Miller said, "and I'll talk when we get back to town."

Clint and Champagne exchanged a glance, and then Champagne said, "Fine, we'll take him back to town. What have we got to lose? It's one less body we have to tie over a horse."

"If you're lying," Clint said to Miller, "you're gonna wish we did leave you out here, dead."

TWENTY-SEVEN

When they rode into Two Forks they attracted a lot of attention because they were trailing four horses with bodies draped over them. They were met at the sheriff's office by Wade Colton, Champagne's temporary deputy, and a bunch of townsmen.

"Wade, have these fellas taken over to the undertaker's office," the sheriff said, handing the deputy the reins to all the horses, including his and the steeldust Clint was riding. "Clint, let's take Mr. Miller inside and get him settled."

"Right."

They walked Miller into the jailhouse and put him in a cell, then Clint and Champagne sat down around the sheriff's office.

"Well," Champagne said, "if the man who hired them is worried, he'll soon know that we have one of the gang in jail."

"And with any luck," Clint said, "he doesn't know which one, which should really worry him."

They'd worked this plan out driving the ride. Even if

Clell Miller didn't know who had hired Ricks, the sixth man didn't know who the live member of the gang was. He would probably take some steps to find out. They figured he would either go to the undertaker's office to view the bodies, or come to the sheriff's office to see who it was. Either way, they'd have him.

"My money's on Dexter," Clint said.

"Are you gonna start that again?" Champagne asked.

"I'm just telling you who I think it is."

"Pete Dexter is the most well-liked man in this town, now that—" He stopped short.

"Go ahead and say it," Clint prodded. "Now that Art Dwyer is gone. You just gave the man another motive."

He got up and walked to the door.

"I need a bath. I'll come back and spell you when I'm done."

"Fine."

"You going to keep your deputy on now that we're back?"

"Yeah," Champagne said, "I usually do when I have a prisoner."

"Okay," Clint said, "that'll leave one of us free to move around. We'll need a man here, a man at the undertaker's, and one on the loose."

They stared at each other with Clint's hand on the door.

"It's not Dexter," Champagne said.

"You really think that?" Clint asked. "Or do you just not want this town to lose Art Dwyer and Pete Dexter in the same week?"

Champagne opened his mouth to answer, but no sound came out.

"Think about it," Clint said, and left.

TWENTY-EIGHT

Clint's hotel room was waiting for him when he got there, but the two girls weren't. The bed was unmade, and the last time he'd been there both girls—Monica and Rachel—had been snuggled together in it. He could still smell them in the room.

He grabbed a fresh shirt and went downstairs for his bath.

Dave McCarthy worked for Pete Dexter and was in town when Clint Adams and Sheriff Tom Champagne came riding in with four dead outlaws and one live one. He immediately got on his horse and rode out to the Dexter ranch to tell his boss the news.

"Four dead, you say?" Pete Dexter asked.

"That's right, Mr. Dexter."

"Do you know who the live one is?"

"I couldn't say," McCarthy answered, "and no one mentioned his name."

Dexter nodded, then said, "Okay, Dave. Thanks. You can go back to work now."

They were standing in front of Dexter's house, and as McCarthy walked away Dexter went up the steps to his porch and stopped there. If the live man was Hal Ricks, he was going to be in trouble. He had to find out who it was. For this he needed his foreman, Bart Heller. He turned around and looked out over his property. There were several men by the corral, one of whom he recognized.

"Frazier!"

"Yeah, boss."

"Find Bart and tell him to come to my office."

"Sure thing, boss. Can I tell him what it's about?"

"If I wanted you to know what it was about," Dexter shouted, "I would have told you. Just find him."

"Right, boss."

It had been Bart Heller who found Hal Ricks. Now it was going to be Bart Heller who found out if Ricks was alive or not.

Dexter went inside to await his foreman.

Clint was soaking in the tub when he heard the door open. He reached for his gun, but stopped when he saw who it was.

"Hello, Clint."

"Hello, Monica," he said. "Where's your friend?"

"Rachel's working," she said, rubbing her hand up and down her arm. "I don't start work until later."

"What brings you here?"

"I heard you were back," she said. "I thought after all that riding that you might need to relax."

"That's what I was doing," Clint said. "Relaxing."

"Well, then," Monica said, her hands plucking at the neckline of her dress, "maybe I'm the one who needs to relax."

Abruptly, the dress fell to the floor and she was naked. She was a big girl, ample and pale, looking like she should be in a frame hanging over a bar in a saloon.

"Ever since you left I been . . . thinkin' about what we did, the three of us," she said.

"And?"

"And I thought that maybe I wanted you for myself for a while."

She cupped her big breasts in each hand and held them out to him, the nipples big and hard.

"Do you want me?"

"If you don't mind a little hot water," he said.

She smiled and said, "I thought you'd never ask," and climbed into the tub with him.

Dexter was waiting in his office, seated behind his desk, when Bart Heller walked in. Heller was a big man who Dexter had hired away from a life of crime a few years back with the promise of big money.

"Heller," Dexter said, "sit down."

"I'll stand, boss."

Of late things had been strained between the two men, because Heller was growing tired of waiting for Dexter to deliver on his big money promises.

"We've got a problem."

"*We* do?"

"As long as you're working for me," Dexter said, "my problems are your problems."

Heller ran one hand thoughtfully over his jaw, then said, "What's the problem?"

"Clint Adams and the sheriff brought in your friend Ricks and his gang today."

"And?"

"Only one of them was left alive."

"Which one?"

"That's what I want to know."

"Ah," Heller said, "if it's Ricks and he talks about who hired him—"

"That's right," Dexter said, "I'll be in trouble. We wouldn't want that, would we?"

"No," Heller said, "I suppose not. What do you want me to do?"

"Find out which member of the gang is still alive."

"And if its Ricks?"

"Kill him before he talks."

"This doesn't come under the heading of foreman duties, does it?" Heller asked.

"No," Dexter said, "this comes under the heading of big money duties."

"How big?"

Dexter named a figure.

"And exactly what do I have to do for that?"

"Make sure Hal Ricks doesn't tell anybody that I hired him."

"And if it isn't Ricks?"

"I don't care who it is," Dexter said, "I don't want him talking. Can I make it any plainer than that?"

"No . . . Boss, that's plain enough."

"So you'll do it?"

"I'll take care of it—"

"Good."

". . . for half up front."

Dexter stared at Heller for a few moments, then said, "Done." He turned, opened his safe, took out a couple of stacks of cash, and tossed them to Heller, who deftly caught them.

"Count it."

"I trust you." Heller put the cash away.

"Now show me I can trust you."

"No problem," Heller said. "I'll leave right away."

Dexter remained behind his desk until the big man's footsteps faded away and he heard the front door close.

When this was all over, he might even have to do something about big Bart Heller.

TWENTY-NINE

Monica's big breasts were slippery when wet and hard to hold in his hands, so Clint brought them to his mouth and sucked the nipples hard. She squealed and reached down into the water for his erect penis. She held it in her hand, then stroked it and finally held it still so she could slide down on it. He entered her easily, and she sat down on him heavily, taking him all the way inside. By this time they had displaced much of the bath water, and what was left was no longer hot.

She began to ride him up and down, splashing what was left of the water out of the tub. Clint would have taken her to his bed if he didn't have to walk through the lobby to get to it.

Her breasts bounced in front of his face and he reached for them and struggled with their slickness again. She put her hands on his shoulders and continued to ride him up and down. Finally, he simply slid his hands beneath her to cup her big buttocks and they bounced against each other like that until Monica cried out and Clint exploded, and the ensuing vibrations almost turned the bathtub over . . .

When she was dried off Clint wanted to grab for her again, but she said, "I have to get dressed and go to work. Besides, somebody might come walkin' in here and catch us."

"What about later tonight?"

She smiled and said, "You want to see me again?"

"Definitely."

"After work, then," she said. "I'll come to your room."

"I'll see you then."

She came to him then and they kissed, and as the kiss deepened he began to become erect again. He slid his hand down to cup her ass cheeks, and she slid her hand down between them and stroked him once, then backed away and headed for the door.

"Better get dressed," she said. "The next person through this door might not be as friendly as me."

As she went out the door he realized she was kidding, but she was also right. He was vulnerable the way he was, and he quickly got dressed and pulled on his clean shirt, then strapped his gun on and left the room.

The next person in there was going to wonder why there was so much water on the floor . . .

"Long bath," Sheriff Champagne said when Clint returned to the sheriff's office.

"I was pretty dirty."

"Clint, this is my part-time deputy, Wade Colton."

The two men shook hands. Colton, who was in his thirties, looked competent enough.

"I usually call Wade in when I have a prisoner, so

he'll be sticking close to the office while Miller is our guest."

"Fine. Glad to be working with you, Wade."

"It's my pleasure, Mr. Adams," Colton said. "I've been hearing about you for a long time. I'm glad to finally get to meet you."

"I just hope when this is all over you won't be sorry you ever met me," Clint said.

"I doubt that."

"Wade, I'm gonna go and get a bath," Champagne said. "Clint or I will be back in a while."

"Is Mr. Adams deputized, Sheriff?" Colton asked.

"No, Wade," Champagne said, "but he might as well be. You do what he says as if the orders were comin' from me. Understand?"

"No," Colton said, "but I'll do it."

"That's what makes you a good deputy, Wade," Champagne said.

He and Clint left the office.

Standing in a doorway across the street was Bart Heller. Chewing on a toothpick, he watched as Clint and the Sheriff left together and walked toward the hotel. That left the part-time deputy, Wade Colton, alone inside with the prisoner.

Heller waited until Clint and Tom Champagne were out of sight, then left his doorway and crossed the street.

Before going for his bath Champagne decided to have a beer in the saloon with Clint.

"When do you figure this sixth man will make his move, Clint?" Champagne asked.

"As far as he's concerned, the sooner the better," Clint said. "I'll go back to the jail after this beer and meet you there later. We should probably move around town in shifts, between the jail and the undertaker."

"I have to pass the undertaker's to get to the hotel to take a bath," Champagne said. "I'll stop in."

"Oh, by the way—" Clint said.

"Yeah."

"When you go to take a bath be careful."

"Why?"

"Somebody made a big mess."

THIRTY

When Clint walked into the sheriff's office he saw Colton, the deputy, with his head down on the desk. He might have thought the man was asleep, but his hat was on his head, sort of. It was at an angle, as if someone had pushed it on there after . . .

Sure enough, when he moved the man his head just sort of rolled on his shoulders. His neck was broken, and he was dead.

One beer, Clint thought, scolding himself.

He went to check the cell, expecting that Miller had either been broken out, or killed. He was lying on his back with his hat over his face.

"Miller."

No answer.

"Miller!"

Still no answer. The man was either dead, or playing possum, but what point was there in killing the deputy if they were going to leave the prisoner untouched.

"What the hell," Clint said, drawing his gun, "I'll put

a bullet in your kneecap, that'll tell me if you're alive or not."

Miller still didn't move.

Clint got the keys off the wall, opened the cell door and entered, keeping his gun ready. When he removed Miller's hat from his face, he holstered his gun. The prisoner was dead, too.

One damn beer . . .

"One beer," Clint said, "I went for one beer and two men are dead."

"What about me?" Champagne said. "I went for a bath."

"I'm the one who said they'd act fast," Clint said, "I just didn't think they'd act this fast. Did he have a family?"

"No, Wade lived alone."

"Like that makes it better," Clint muttered.

They were sitting in the office, passing a bottle of whiskey back and forth.

"So much for out great plan," Champagne said.

"Go on and say it," Clint told him, "my plan."

"Our plan," the lawman said. "I went along with it, didn't I?"

"I got your man killed."

"Cut it out," Champagne said. "He knew the risks of wearing the job."

"Yeah," Clint said, "no part-time risks, though. He's full-time dead, now."

"Cut it out . . ." Champagne said, again.

They sat in silence for a while, cutting into the level of the bottle . . .

* * *

"We got them, though," the lawman said, then.

"What?"

"We got them," Champagne said, "the sons of bitches who killed Art Dwyer. We got 'em."

"But we didn't get the man who hired them," Clint said. "And we don't know where Ramona is."

"Maybe," Champagne said, "she's where she wants to be."

"I had the feeling that if I said that you would have took a shot at me," Clint said.

"You mean you were thnkin' it, too?"

"Yep."

More silence, more drinking . . .

"Do you still think it's Dexter?" Champagne asked later.

"Yes."

"Why?"

"He just had the most to gain."

"And you think he walked in here and broke two men's necks?" the sheriff asked.

"Maybe," Clint said, "or he had it done, just like he had Art Dwyer burned out and killed."

"There are half a dozen other ranchers who could have done the same thing."

"Okay," Clint said, "then let's go and see them."

"All of them?"

"Why not? We'll question them all and see how you feel when we're done," Clint suggested.

"I can't just ride up to the ranchers in the county and ask them if they had Art Dwyer killed."

"Are you afraid of losing your job?"

Champagne didn't answer.

"Look, Tom," Clint said, "I really am not asking you to risk your job. You know what? I'll do it. I'll go out and question them all, but I really think Dexter's the man."

"If you start bothering the ranchers," Champagne said, "they're gonna come to me to stop you. That'll put us on opposite sides of the fence, Clint."

"Then what do you want to do?"

"We got the men who killed Art Dwyer," Champagne said. "Maybe we should be satisfied with that."

"And what about your deputy?" Clint asked. "Who killed him? Don't you want to know that?"

"Sure, I do," the sheriff said, "but I'm not a detective."

"Then call in federal help," Clint said. "Call in a federal marshal to investigate the death of your deputy."

"That makes sense," Tom Champagne said. "Will you back off, then, if I do that?"

"Oh, no," Clint said.

"Why not?"

"Because a federal man will investigate your man's murder," Clint said, "while I'm still looking for the man who had Art Dwyer murdered."

"And you think the two are connected."

"Definitely," Clint said. "What reason would somebody have to kill your deputy?"

"Maybe he got somebody mad at him."

"And why kill the prisoner?"

"Maybe he saw who killed Wade."

Clint passed Tom Champagne the bottle with the last of the whiskey in it and stood up.

"Where are you going?"

"I can't talk to you anymore tonight," Clint said. "Maybe tomorrow you'll make more sense."

"Me make more sense?" Champagne called out as Clint walked to the door. "I'm not the one accusing the richest man in the county of murder."

"Maybe you should be," Clint said, and left.

THIRTY-ONE

Clint was only in his room a few minutes when there was a knock at the door. He'd forgotten that Monica was going to come over after work. He remembered the bath, and was glad she was there. He needed the distraction—and pleasure—her body offered. She was one woman who definitely had a body that was built for a man to enjoy.

He opened the door and saw Rachel standing there, not Monica. She was dressed for work in a low-cut saloon dress but was holding a shawl tightly around her.

"Can I come in?"

"Uh, sure," he said, "by all means."

She walked past him and the scent of her tickled his nose. He wondered how she would react when Monica showed up, or how Monica would react when she arrived and found Rachel there. After all, they *were* very close friends.

"You weren't expecting me," she said, removing her shawl and tossing it aside. Her skin was a little darker than Monica's, but no less smooth looking. Rachel was taller, more slender, with long legs and high breasts that were shaped like ripe—make that overripe—peaches.

"Uh, no," he said. "I was just getting ready to turn in."

"Was it terrible for you?" she asked. "Having to kill all those men?"

"Yes," he said, "killing is always terrible."

She came close to him and put her hands on his shoulders.

"I can make you forget all about that," she said.

He noticed that she had a full, ripe mouth, with the upper lips as full as the lower. Monica's lips were thinner, her mouth wider. Both women were very different, each attractive and appealing in her own way. He found himself wondering how Rachel would have looked in the bathtub this afternoon.

"Clint."

"What?"

"Take off your clothes."

He did.

"Now take off mine."

He did that, too. While Monica's nipples were a pale pink, Rachel's were a dark brown. It was quite a contrast, one he hadn't really had time to ponder when all three of them had been together.

She laced her fingers behind his head and pulled his head down to hers so she could kiss him. First, however, she ran her tongue over his lips, first the bottom, then the top. Then she took his bottom lip between her teeth and sucked it into her mouth—and then she kissed him. Rachel, it seemed, liked to be a little more in control than Monica, who was happy to do whatever a man wanted, or to let a man do whatever he wanted to her.

She slid her hands down his back until she was cupping the cheeks of his ass, then she turned him around and got down on her knees. She rubbed her face over his butt, then ran her tongue along the crease between his cheeks. Finally, she bit him on the left buttock.

"Ouch!"

"You were with Monica this afternoon, weren't you?" she asked. She ran her long nails along the shaft of his penis. "Don't lie."

"Yes, I was," he said. "She came—"

"She's very good, isn't she?" Rachel asked. "I mean, at pleasing a man, she's very good."

"Yes."

"I'm very good, too."

"I'm sure."

"But in a different way."

"Yes."

"Would you like me to show you?"

"Yes."

"And you'll do whatever I say?"

"Yes."

She stood up and turned him around.

"Is she coming here after work?"

"Yes."

"Good," she said, taking hold of his penis and using it to tug him toward the bed, "I'll try not to tire you out too much . . ."

Later, when there was a knock on the door, Rachel said, "I'll get it . . ."

She dismounted, leaving Clint's penis slick with her juices and cold when the night air hit it. It was the third time he had been inside of her. He watched her tight butt twitch as she walked to the door. Monica's butt was bigger, wider—everything about Rachel seemed to bring to mind peaches, while everything about Monica seemed to bring to mind pears.

Luckily, Clint liked all kinds of fruit.

Rachel opened the door, completely naked, and leaned against it, one hand on the door and one on her hip.

Standing in the hallway was Monica.

"Whore," Monica said.

"Bitch," Rachel said.

Monica leaned forward and sniffed Rachel, then licked the sweat off her shoulder.

"You know I can't resist you when you sweat," she said.

Rachel took one of Monica's hands and drew her inside the room, closing the door behind them. She drew her to the bed and Clint was amazed that somewhere between the door and the bed, Monica had lost all her clothes.

"Now where were we?" Rachel asked Clint.

Dexter was awake when the knocking started on the front door of his house. In fact, he had just come up from the root cellar, where he had been talking to Ramona Dwyer and, in fact, giving her something to eat. She had, indeed, begun to eat, unable to resist the hunger any longer, but she still refused to speak to him.

Dexter had to answer the door himself because he did not have any family living with him—and, in fact, did not have any family period—and did not allow servants in the house.

He opened the door and Bart Heller said, "It wasn't Ricks."

"Who was it?"

"Fella named Clell Miller."

"I remember him," Dexter said. "Will he talk?"

"Never again."

"Good. So Ricks is dead?"

"Very."

"Excellent," Dexter said. "You did a good job, Bart."

"Maybe not."

"What do you mean?"

"I had to kill another man, too."

"Who?"

"A deputy."

"Was it unavoidable?"

"Oh, yeah, it was unavoidable," Heller said. Sure, he thought, that was a good way to put it.

"Then it doesn't matter," Dexter said. "You did fine. Good night." He started to close the door, but Heller stopped it with the heel of his hand.

"What?" Dexter said.

"The rest of my money?"

"Now?"

"Yes."

"Don't you trust me?"

"Sure."

"But you still want it now?"

"Yes."

Dexter studied the bigger, younger man for a moment, then started to laugh, shaking his head.

"I knew there was a reason I liked you, Bart," he said. "You have the heart of a businessman."

"Should I take that as a compliment?"

"Why don't you come inside," Dexter said, "and we'll try to figure that out while I get your money."

THIRTY-TWO

Once again Clint Adams awoke wedged between two beautiful bodies. They were also two *hot* bodies, giving off so much heat that he *peeled* away from them more than pulled away. So much had gone on during the night, though, that both women were exhausted, and did not wake as Clint worked his way out from between them and got out of bed. As soon as he was gone, though, they both moaned and rolled toward each other, snuggling together. It was then that Clint wondered if something wasn't going on in the bed while he was asleep, if these two girls weren't, in fact, wearing each other out while he slept.

He preferred not to think that he slept that soundly.

He dressed and went downstairs in search of a decent breakfast, something he had not had for days.

Clint was having breakfast in a small café when Sheriff Tom Champagne found him.

"Mind if I sit?" Champagne asked.

"To eat?"

127

"To apologize."

Clint waved at the other chair and said, "But only if you also eat."

"Deal."

Before long they both had plates in front of them with steak and eggs and potatoes on them.

"I'm sorry about last night," the lawman said. "I was drunk and was looking for a way out."

"That's okay."

"Naw, it's not."

"Then let's just pretend that it is, all right?"

"Sure," Champagne said. "You're makin' it easy on me."

"That's what friends are for."

They ate in silence for a few moments before Champagne broke it.

"Dexter has a man named Bart Heller workin' for him."

Clint put down his fork.

"Why does that name ring a bell?"

"He was an outlaw for a while."

"And what happened?"

"Dexter hired him," Champagne said, "promised to pay him more than he could make as an outlaw, I guess."

"Hired him as what?"

"Foreman."

"But the man still has certain . . . talents that Dexter can make use of when he needs to?"

"That's what I'm sayin'."

"And is one of those talents . . . murder?"

"That I don't know," Champagne said. "I've known Heller to beat a man to within an inch of his life a time or to, probably under orders from Dexter, but murder . . . I just haven't seen that."

"Is it in his past?"

"Not that I know of."

"What kind of man is he?"

"A big man," Champagne said.

"Big enough to break someone's neck with his hands?"

"Plenty big enough for that."

"So maybe we should have a talk with Mr. Heller?"

"And ask around to see if anyone saw him in town yesterday about the time of the killing?"

Clint gave Champagne a look and said, "And you claim that you're not a detective."

THIRTY-THREE

After breakfast Clint and Champagne saddled their horses—Clint still using the steeldust—and rode out to Pete Dexter's ranch. When they arrived men were working in the corral with some horses and a couple over by the barn. They rode their horses up to the front of the house and Pete Dexter himself came out to greet them. He had heard the approaching horses and came out to see who was calling on him.

"Well," he said, "the sheriff and the Gunsmith. Is it my lucky day or my unlucky day?"

"Don't rightly know, Mr. Dexter," Tom Champagne said. "We came out looking for your foreman, Heller."

Dexter made a show of looking around, then looked back up at Clint and Champagne.

"Don't see him," he said. "What's this about?"

"We just need to ask him a few questions," Champagne said.

"We? Is the Gunsmith one of your deputies now, Sheriff?"

"Mr. Adams is just helping me with some inquiries,

131

Mr. Dexter," the lawman said. "Can you give me some idea where Heller might be?"

"He could be any number of places," Dexter said, "but let me talk to my men and see if I can find out exactly where. You see, I want to cooperate in any way I can."

"Well, I'm much obliged for the help, sir," Champagne said.

Dexter walked over to the corral and the men, who had stopped working to watch, suddenly got busy again. They stopped again, though, when he reached them and started talking to them. Once he was done talking, though, they got back to work and he walked back to where Clint and Tom Champagne were waiting.

"Seems we have some fence problems that my foreman is looking into," Dexter said. "Let me give you directions on where and how to find him . . ."

After they got the directions Champagne said, "Thanks a lot, Mr. Dexter."

"Is he in some kind of trouble?" Dexter asked. "Get in a fight, break some furniture, or something?"

"Was he here last night, Mr. Dexter?" Clint asked. "Or was he in town? Do you know?"

"To tell you the truth, Mr. Adams, I don't," Dexter said. "I'm afraid I don't keep that close a watch on my men when they're on their own time."

"I see."

"We'll go and talk to Heller, Mr. Dexter," Champagne said. "Come on, Clint."

"Do me a favor, Sheriff, will you?" Dexter asked.

"Of course."

"Don't keep him from his work too long, if you don't have to."

"Well do our best, sir."

"I'd be much obliged," Dexter said.

Clint and Champagne turned their horses and rode off.

"That's was ugly," Clint said, when they were out of sight of the ranch.

"What was?"

"All that yes, sir and no, sir," Clint said.

"That's the way I treat people, Clint," Champagne said. "If I didn't talk to him that way he'd get suspicious."

"Good point, Sheriff," Clint said. "I'm sorry. It's just that—"

"Just that what?"

"I'm more convinced than ever that it's him," Clint said.

"What did you see that I didn't?"

"He just seemed to be laughing at us the whole time," Clint said. "Didn't you get that impression?"

"Actually," Champagne said, "no, I didn't."

"Well," Clint said, "I did."

Dexter waited until the two riders were out of sight and then called over a man named Martinez.

"Do you know exactly where Heller is?"

"Si, Patron."

"English, damn it."

"Yes, I do, Boss."

"Well, you ride out and tell him he's got company coming," Dexter said, "The sheriff and the Gunsmith."

"Hijo de cabron," the man said, "one of those men was the Gunsmith?"

"Yes, it was," Dexter said. "Now you get out to Heller and tell him, all right?"

"Si—I mean, yes, sir. I will."

"And take the most direct route," Dexter said. "I just sent those men on a little detour."

"Yes," Martinez said. "I will go now."

"And hurry."

As Martinez ran to the livery to saddle his horse Dexter knew he was going to have to do something about Adams. The man would never rest until he found out who ordered Art Dwyer's death, and the way he was looking at Dexter the rancher was sure Adams thought he knew something.

THIRTY-FOUR

"Something's wrong," Clint said.

"Like what?"

Clint had reined the steeldust in, and Champagne followed.

"Dexter must think we have no sense of direction," Clint said. "He sent us a long way around."

Champagne looked around, stood in his stirrups, then sat back down in his saddle.

"You're right," he said. "So he sent somebody to warn Heller that we were coming."

"Yeah, but warn him about what?" Clint asked. "We didn't tell Dexter what we wanted to talk to him about."

Champagne rubbed his jaw.

"So that means he already knew."

"Ah," Clint said, "you're coming around to my way of thinking, now."

"Maybe," Champagne said. "There's not much we can do about it now, though. Let's go ahead and find Heller and hear what he has to say."

"Let's go this way," Clint said. "It'll be shorter . . ."

•   •   •

Bart Heller looked up from what he was doing, as did the two men with him. They had all been working on a fence post, but were now watching a rider approach.

"Who is it?" one man asked.

"Looks like Martinez," the other said.

"What's he in such an all fired hurry about?" the first man asked.

"You two keep workin'," Heller said, "and I'll find out."

Heller walked away from the two men so that when he did talk with Martinez they wouldn't be able hear.

Martinez reined his horse in and dismounted. Heller approached him.

"What's wrong, Martinez?"

"Señor Dexter sent me to warn you."

"About what?"

"Two men are coming to see you."

"Out here?"

"*Si*. One is *el jefe*, the sheriff, and the other is—"

"In English, Martinez," Heller said, sensing that the man had been about to lapse back into Spanish.

"The Gunsmith," Martinez said, his tone low.

"Did Mr. Dexter say what it was about?"

"No, he did not. Only that I should come very quickly and warn you."

"All right," Heller said, "you warned me. Now get out of here before somebody sees you."

Martinez mounted his horse, turned it, and rode off as fast as he had come.

"What was that about?" one of the men asked.

"Just keep workin'," Heller said. "We're gonna have some company."

•   •   •

"There!" Clint said. "A rider."

Champagne saw him, riding hell bent for leather back toward the ranch.

"Guess he must've delivered his message already."

"I guess so," Clint said. "Come on, Heller should be just over that rise."

When Heller saw Clint and Champagne top the rise and start down he told the men, "Just keep workin', I'll handle this."

"Okay, boss."

One of two things was going to happen, Heller figured. Either they were just going to ask him some questions, or Dexter had panicked and given him up. He didn't think that was the case, though, because he'd never known Pete Dexter to panic. He decided just to play innocent and wait for the questions.

"What good is this going to do?" Clint complained, as they approached Heller and the two men who were working on fence posts with him.

"What do you mean?"

"He's already been warned," Clint said. "we're not going to get anything out of him he doesn't want to give us."

"Maybe questioning him will rattle him," Champagne said.

"I don't know the man and you do, Sheriff," Clint said. "Do you think he'll rattle?"

"Not likely."

"Great."

"Maybe just one of us should do the talking," Champagne said.

"You've got the badge," Clint said. "You talk to him

and I'll just stare at him. Maybe that'll rattle him."

"And if it doesn't?"

"Well, at least he'll know that we thought to come out and question him," Clint said.

"My mother used to tell me to be grateful for small favors," Champagne said. "I guess this is what she meant."

THIRTY-FIVE

"Bart Heller?" Tom Champagne asked.

"That's right," Heller said. "You're Tom Champagne, right?"

"Sheriff Champagne."

"Right, Sheriff," Heller said. "I see you around town." He looked at Clint. "You I ain't seen."

"He hasn't been here that long," Champagne said.

"Deputy?"

"No," the sheriff said, "he's just helpin' me out on some things."

Clint continued to stare at Heller.

"He don't talk?" Heller asked.

"Not much."

Clint thought Heller was going to take exception to being stared at, but abruptly the man turned his attention solely to the lawman.

"Well, I got work to do here, Sheriff," he said, "so if you got somethin' you want to talk to me about?"

"Were you in town yesterday, Mr. Heller?"

"Let me think," Heller said. "When yesterday?"

"Any time will do."

"Well," Heller said, "I think I was there in the afternoon—musta been after you brought in them dead men, though. "I didn't see that. Musta been a sight, huh?"

"So you were there after that?"

"I guess."

"And how long did you stay?"

"Can't say."

"Why not?"

"Can't recall."

"Was it dark when you left?"

Heller made a show of thinking, then said, "Mighta been."

"You can't remember if it was dark when you left town to go back to the ranch?"

"I guess I'd been drinkin' some. What's this about, anyway?"

"My deputy got himself killed yesterday."

"That's a damn shame," Heller said. He looked at Clint again, finally. "Is that why he keeps starin' at me? 'Cause he thinks I done it?"

"I don't know why he does what he does, Mr. Heller," the sheriff said. "I never ask him."

Heller snapped his fingers.

"I know who you are," he said to Clint. "You're the Gunsmith. I heard you was in town."

Clint didn't answer.

"I didn't hear that you don't talk, though," Heller said. "Nope, I surely didn't hear that." He looked at Champagne again. "Is that all, Sheriff, 'cause I got lots of fence posts to work on."

"Did you see anyone near the sheriff's office last night, Mr. Heller?" Champagne asked.

"Well," Heller said, "I don't rightly know that I was

anywhere near the sheriff's office, Sheriff. Ya see, I ain't never been there."

"It's right close to the saloon."

"Which saloon," Heller said. "There's a few in town, ain't there?"

"Well," Champagne said, "I'll bet if I tell you what saloon it's near you'll tell me that you were at one of the other ones, won't you?"

"Sheriff," Heller said, "you make it sound like I ain't tryin' ta help, and ain't I answerin' all your questions to the best of my ability?"

"I hope you are, Mr. Heller," Champagne said, "because if I find out you aren't, I'm afraid my friend and I will have to come back and see you again."

"Is that a threat?" Heller asked.

"A promise," Clint said.

Heller looked at him, surprised that he'd spoken.

Clint smiled at him, wheeled the steeldust around and rode off with Champagne close behind.

"What was that about, Bart?" one of the man asked.

"Nothin'," Heller said, "not a damn thing."

"What do you think?" Champagne asked Clint as they rode back to town.

"I got the same feeling from him I got from his boss," Clint said. "That he was laughing at us."

"Well," the lawman said, "this time I got the same feelin' right along with you—and I didn't like it much."

"We'll have to check the saloons and see which one he was at," Clint said, "if he was even at any of them."

"Oh, he was in town, all right," Champagne said.

"How do you know?"

"Because he didn't lie about it," the sheriff said. "If he lied we might find somebody who saw him, and then we'd catch him in the lie. So he told us he was in town, he just can't remember when he left, or where he was while he was there."

"Convenient."

"Yeah."

"That's pretty good thinking, though."

"Thanks."

They rode in silence for a few moments and then Clint added, "Just like a real detective."

THIRTY-SIX

When Bart Heller returned to the Dexter ranch he went right to the house to see Pete Dexter.

"I've been expecting you," Dexter said, as he let the man in.

"I guess I should thank you for the warning," Heller said. "What did they ask you?"

"Just where you were," Dexter replied.

"Did they say why?"

"They wanted to ask you some questions. Did they?"

"About the deputy gettin' killed and about bein' in town yesterday," Heller said. "That is, the sheriff did the askin'. That Adams didn't talk at all until right at the end, and then he only said two words."

"They were tryin' to unnerve you."

"Make me nervous, you mean?" Heller asked. "Well, they did that. Why are they askin' us about this? What do they know?"

"They don't know anything," Dexter said. "If they were able to prove anything they would have arrested us. All we have to do is keep our nerve, Bart. We can't let them rattle us."

"Us?" Heller repeated. "You mean, us like we're partners?"

"Partners?" Dexter laughed. "Now, don't get carried away, Bart. I'm going to pay you real well for all this, but partners . . ." Dexter shook his head.

"Maybe you're right," Heller said. "I mean, why would I want all the headaches of bein' a partner? I can just work for you and make a lot of money with no worries."

"That's right."

"Unless I get put in jail for committing murder for you!"

"Nobody's going to jail," Dexter said. "I guarantee that."

"You do, huh?"

"This is all going to blow over," Dexter said, "just wait and see. There's just one other thing we have to do."

"And what's that?"

"We have to get rid of the Gunsmith."

"You mean, like, make him leave town?" Heller asked.

Dexter smiled and said, "I think you know what I mean, Bart."

"Look," Heller said, "as long as he's wearin' a gun I ain't goin' anywhere near him."

"Then we'll just have to find a way to get to him when he's not wearing a gun."

"And when would that be?"

"Well," Dexter said, scratching his head, "I guess when he's in bed, either with a woman or asleep. Does he have a woman in town?"

"How would I know that?"

"We know he has to sleep," Dexter said. "Can you . . . set this up? Get the right men for it?"

"By right men you mean men who will kill for money."

"Bart," Dexter said, "you have an annoying habit of having to put everything so bluntly."

"I just don't want to make any mistakes, Mr. Dexter," Heller said. "I'm sure you can appreciate that."

"Oh yes," Dexter said, "I appreciate that about you, very much, Bart. We wouldn't want to make any mistakes—like killing a deputy."

"I was wondering when that was going to come up," Heller said. "I told you that was unavoidable. If you wanted Miller dead, the deputy had to go."

"All right, all right," Dexter said, holding up his hands, "there's no use arguing over what's done. Okay, let's put this very plainly, then. The Gunsmith needs to die, and soon."

"And the sheriff?" Heller asked. "Is he just gonna forget about the death of his deputy?"

"As a matter of fact," Pete Dexter said, "without Clint Adams around for him to lean on, I think he just might."

"All right," Heller said. "I can make arrangements for Adams to be dealt with."

"Dealt with?" Dexter said, chuckling. "Now who's not talking plain?"

THIRTY-SEVEN

"You want to do what?" Sheriff Tom Champagne asked.

"I want to get into Pete Dexter's house and have a look around."

They had returned from talking with Bart Heller, left their horses at the livery, and gone directly to the saloon closest to the sheriff's office.

"You want to break in?"

"That's right."

"How are you going to get close to it?" Champagne asked. "He has a lot of men working for him."

"They all have to sleep, don't they?"

Champagne sat back in his chair and took a swig of his beer.

"I can't go with you, you know."

"I know."

"I'd definitely lose my job if I got caught breaking into somebody's house."

Clint supposed he couldn't fault the lawman for constantly worrying about his job. He'd been a lawman long enough to know that your livelihood depends on satisfying the people who elected you, or hired you. That was why he couldn't do it, anymore.

"I don't expect you to go with me."

"And if he catches you and brings you to me, I'll have to lock you up," Champagne went on.

"Tom," Clint said, "if I'm right, and he catches me, he'll probably have me killed. You won't have to arrest me."

"Well . . . good," Champagne said, toying with his beer mug. "That makes me feel better."

"Look, I'm just going to walk around a bit, see if anybody remembers seeing Heller in town yesterday."

"And when are you gonna . . . you know, do it?"

"Break into his house?"

"Shhh," the sheriff said, looking around. It was still pretty early and there weren't that many men in the saloon. Eddie, the bartender, was wiping down the bar and didn't seem to have heard.

"You know what, Tom?" Clint said, lowering his voice to suit the lawman. "I won't tell you when I'm going to do it, so you won't be nervous about it. How about that?"

"That suits me," Champagne said. "You know, I never knew *I* was the nervous type until all this started."

"That's okay, Tom," Clint said. "We all get nervous sometime."

"Even you?"

"Oh, yeah," Clint said, "even me."

After Champagne left the saloon and went back to his office Clint started his inquiries with the bartender, Eddie.

"Sure, I know Bart Heller."

"Was he in here yesterday, at any time?"

"Mmmm, not that I can think of," Eddie said.

"Was there a time when you weren't tending bar?"

"Nope," Eddie said. "I couldn't find a relief bartender yesterday, so I was working all day. That's what happens when you own a place."

"So you're saying he definitely wasn't in here."

"I'm saying I didn't serve him a drink," Eddie corrected. "Now, maybe he sat at a table when it was crowded and got a drink from one of the girls. I can ask them, if you want."

"Yeah, do that, and thanks," Clint said. "Does he drink anywhere else in town?"

"I don't know, maybe," Eddie said, with a shrug. "When somebody needs a drink they ain't exactly loyal to one saloon, ya know? They usually just go to the nearest one."

"Right," Clint said. "Okay, thanks. I'll check back in with you later, after you've talked to your girls."

"Yeah," Eddie said, "unless you talk to my girls first."

Clint checked in with the other two saloons in town, and none of the bartenders he spoke to remembered seeing Bart Heller, although they all knew him on sight.

"Foreman of the biggest ranch hereabouts," one of the bartenders said, "sure I know him on sight."

So it was beginning to look like Heller lied about being in town and drinking too much—unless somebody had bought him a bottle and he drank it out on the street.

Clint tried to think where else Heller might have gone, but decided that asking any more questions might get back to the man. Then he decided maybe that wouldn't be such a bad idea. If Heller came after him, that would be as good as a confession of guilt.

So he walked all over town, asking everyone he came to if they knew Bart Heller, if they had seen him the day before. He even stopped into the local cathouse, fought off a couple of the girls, and asked if they'd seen Heller yesterday. The answer was no.

Nobody had seen him all day.

If he had come into town he'd done so without anyone knowing and had killed the deputy and Clell Miller.

"Of course," Tom Champagne told him later, when he finished explaining how he'd spent his day, "there's another possibility."

"And what's that?"

"That nobody saw him in town because he *wasn't* in town and *didn't* kill anyone."

"Well, yeah," Clint said, grudgingly, "that's a possibility."

THIRTY-EIGHT

Fifteen miles from Two Forks was a small town called Springville. For a town with a benign name, however, it was home to men who were too well known, or wanted, for them to walk into a larger town like Two Forks whenever they wanted a drink or a meal. This was where Bart Heller had found Hal Ricks and his men when Pete Dexter told him he needed some men for a "special" job.

This was the kind of town Bart Heller was headed for when Pete Dexter offered him the job as foreman of his ranch.

When Heller came to Springville, it reminded him how fortunate he was that he'd been smart enough to take that job, even if it hadn't exactly turned out the way he thought it would. Still, it was better than this . . .

He entered the only saloon in Springville and all eyes were on him as he walked to the bar. They recognized him, though, as one of them—or as a man who used to be one of them—and ignored him after a few moments.

"Whataya have?" the bartender asked.

"Beer."

When the man brought the beer he asked, "Ain't you the fella was in here a while back and hired Hal Ricks to do a job."

"That's right."

"I heard Ricks got killed."

"I guess he didn't do the job right."

"Guess not," the bartender said, and drifted away to another end of the bar.

Heller took his beer, turned and surveyed the room. There was a good chance that every man in the place had, at one time or another, killed someone.

Now he just needed to find someone who also had an ounce of brains.

Clint was in the saloon where Rachel and Monica worked, Eddie behind the bar. The two girls were working the same hours tonight, and he watched them move around the room.

"They're gonna kill you, you know," Eddie said to him.

"What?"

"Those two," Eddie said, "if you keep it up, they'll wear you out and end up killin' you—but what a way to go, huh?"

"Yeah," Clint said, wondering how Eddie knew about him and the two saloon girls.

"They must like you a lot," the bartender said. "They don't usually do it for free."

Not only did he know about them, he knew that Clint wasn't paying. But then he was a bartender. Bartenders knew a lot. He wondered if Eddie knew some things that he wasn't telling, but decided that wasn't the case. One of the reasons bartenders knew so much was that they talked so much. Whatever they found out, they were always in a hurry to tell it to somebody else. In that respect, Clint thought they were worse than barbers.

"They're gonna be workin' late tonight," Eddie said. "What're you gonna do with yourself?"

"Guess I'll turn in," Clint said. He pushed the half empty mug of beer over to Eddie. "Good night."

"Want me to give them a message?"

"Nope," Clint said, and left the saloon.

Heller had managed to find three men who didn't mind killing for money, but he'd had to give up on the ounce of brains—they did have one ounce among them.

Which was why they screwed up, miserably.

They had gotten into the hotel all right, and they had even found Clint's room, but they hadn't been able to get the door open. One of them wanted to kick it open, but the other one said that the man they were supposed to kill might notice that his door was broken when he came back.

Of course, they didn't know who they were trying to kill. Heller had decided to keep that little piece of information from them.

So while they were trying to get his door open, the door to one of the other rooms opened up and a man called out, "Can't you be quiet? Some people are tryin' to sleep."

"Go to hell," one of the hired killers called back, and the three men went back to trying to get the door unlocked.

The other guest decided to go to the front desk and complain about all the noise.

•   •   •

"They're tryin' to do what?" the clerk was asking a man as Clint entered the lobby of the hotel.

"They're tryin' to get the door to their room open," the guest said. "Why don't you just give them another key?"

Clint was heading for the stairs when the clerk asked, "What room are they trying to get into?"

"It's room twelve."

Clint stopped with his foot on the first step. Room twelve was his room. He withdrew his foot and walked over to the front desk.

"Go and get the sheriff," he said.

"Hey, I was here fir—" the guest started to complain.

"Now!" Clint said.

THIRTY-NINE

The clerk and the guest both left the hotel and went in search of the sheriff. Clint went to the stairs again and this time he put his foot on the first step gingerly. He knew he should wait for the sheriff, but there was no telling what the three men in the hall would do. While they were in the hall there was a good chance they'd get in each other's way. If they managed to get down to the lobby they'd have more room to maneuver. Besides, one lawman was dead already. Clint decided he could take care of this himself, without risking injury to Sheriff Champagne. After all, if it wasn't for one beer, that deputy might still be alive.

He put his foot on the second step and started up the stairs as quietly as he could. Even before he reached the top he could hear the men in the hallway, cursing the locked door.

He reached the top and paused before sticking his head around the corner and taking a look. Sure enough, three men were hunched over his door lock, trying to

get it open so they could wait for him and—no doubt—
kill him.

He stepped into the hall.

"Hey," he called, "that's my room."

All three men turned and looked at him. They went
for their guns and, sure enough, two of them got their
arms tangled. Clint drew and fired, hitting the third man
in the shoulder and putting him down on the floor. The
other two stared at him.

"It's up to you," Clint said. "Go for your guns or drop
them."

"Kill 'im," the wounded man said through clenched
teeth.

But the other two men weren't as anxious. After all,
he was *facing* them *and* he had his gun out.

They dropped their guns to the floor.

"Okay," Clint said, "let's go downstairs and wait for
the sheriff. Help your friend up.

The two men helped up the wounded one and walked
him down the hall. Clint allowed the men to precede
him down the stairs, and when they reached the lobby
Sheriff Champagne came running in with the clerk and
the other guest behind him.

"Looks like you've got things under control," the
sheriff said.

"Got some guests for your jail," Clint said.

"Good," the guest said, "does this mean I can go back
to sleep?"

Clint looked at the guest and said, "That's exactly
what it means."

When the three men were in a cell the sheriff sent for
the doctor to look at the wounded one. They waited

while the doctor patched him up, then went in to talk to the three of them.

"You boys are in a lot of trouble," Champagne said.

"For what?" the wounded one asked. "Tryin' to get into our room? We lost our key."

"That was my room," Clint said.

"So we had the wrong room."

"The desk clerk says that none of you is a guest in the hotel," Champagne told them.

"So we had the wrong hotel," the wounded man said. "We had too much to drink."

"You drew on me," Clint said. "That's attempted murder."

"Self-defense," the man said. "We didn't know who you were. We thought you was tryin' to rob us."

"A judge ain't gonna buy that," Champagne said.

"Come on," Clint said, "all you boys have to do is tell us who hired you to kill me."

"And then what?" the wounded man—apparently the leader—asked. "You'll let us go?"

"I can't do that," the sheriff said, "but I'll tell the judge you cooperated with us. Maybe get you a reduced sentence."

"We ain't talkin'," the wounded man said, but Clint saw the other two men exchange glances.

"We'll let you think about it for a while," Clint said, "maybe talk it over a bit."

He and Champagne went back into the office.

"What do you think?" the lawman asked.

"Dexter hired them," Clint said, "probably through Heller."

Champagne rubbed his jaw and said, "I think you're right."

"Sorry, Tom," Clint said. "I know you didn't want it to be Dexter."

"I don't know if this town can survive losing two men like Art Dwyer and Pete Dexter, Clint," Champagne said. "They brought in a lot of business."

"I know."

"Maybe it was Heller workin' on his own."

"Maybe."

"You don't believe that."

"No," Clint said, "and neither do you."

"No," Champagne said, "I guess I don't."

Clint headed for the door.

"Just keep asking them questions," he suggested. "One of them will crack."

"Where are you going?"

Clint opened the door and said, "You don't want to know."

FORTY

Clint saddled the steeldust and rode out to within half a mile of the Dexter ranch. He didn't want to get any closer that that because he couldn't trust the horse to keep quiet. If he'd had Duke, he would have ridden to within yards of the place, knowing that the big gelding would not make a sound.

He walked the half a mile, and when he reached the ranch house, he saw lights. There were also lights in the bunkhouse. The livery stable, however, was dark, so he worked his way to it and settled down against one wall to wait out the lights.

"You hired three idiots?" Dexter asked.

"They were the best I could find on short notice."

"If they get caught they'll talk."

"They don't know anything about you."

"No, but they know about you, and you work for me."

"They don't know my name."

Dexter turned and stared out the window of his office. He did that for a few moments before turning back.

"All right," he said, "let's wait and see what morning brings. If we get lucky, they'll get lucky and kill him."

"You said you wanted this done fast."

"If this doesn't work," Dexter said, pointing a finger at Heller, "I want you to do it yourself."

"I can do that," Heller said, "as long as I don't have to face him with a gun. Hand to hand, I'll be able to do it."

"I don't care how you do it," Dexter said, "I just want it done. Now go and get some sleep. I'm going to do the same."

"I'll check in with you in the morning."

"Do that."

Heller left the office and the house and walked to the bunkhouse.

Dexter doused the light, left the office, went to the kitchen and lit a lamp there. He unlocked the doors to the root cellar, lit a second lamp and took it down with him.

Ramona Dwyer stared at him from her corner. She was still wearing the same clothes she was wearing the day her husband was killed. He could still smell the smoke on her from the fire. Her hair was a mess, all tangled and dirty, and she was still beautiful to him. He didn't care what her past had been, all he knew was that when she first arrived in town he'd wanted her and she had chosen Dwyer. First Dwyer got the army contract to supply horses to the cavalry, and then he'd gotten Ramona. That was twice he had beaten Pete Dexter, and Dexter had sworn there would not be a third time.

"I came to say good night," he said to her.

She was not gagged, for she had learned that screaming did no good. No one could hear her. However, she did not speak to him.

"Ramona," he said, "all you have to do is say good night to me and you can have a bath."

She didn't reply.

"Don't you want a bath?"

No answer.

"This can't go on," he said. "You have to speak to me sooner or later."

She didn't reply.

"Damn you, woman!" he snapped. "You will not beat me. No one beats me—*ever*."

She was tempted to say, *"Art beat you, my husband beat you,"* but she didn't. She just glared at him.

Dexter took a deep breath and said, "All right, fine. I can wait. I have plenty of time."

He turned and went back up the steps. He doused the lamp and hung it on a hook, then closed the doors of the root cellar. Then he took the other lamp and carried it with him to his room—a room he would soon be sharing with her. He got into the bed he would soon share with her. She couldn't hold out forever.

No one could.

Clint watched as the light moved around the house. He knew from Tom Champagne that Pete Dexter lived in his house alone and had no one working for him. A man like that wouldn't trust anyone in his house with him.

The light disappeared, then appeared at an upstairs window. Clint waited, retracing the movements of the light in his head, and then it finally went out altogether.

He'd seen Heller leave, had seen the light move, probably from Dexter's office to another room. Which one? The kitchen? Maybe. And then it had moved from there upstairs, undoubtedly to a bedroom.

If Ramona Dwyer was in that house, was she upstairs or somewhere downstairs?

Was she willing or unwilling?

All he had to do to prove that Dexter was behind this whole thing was find Ramona Dwyer in his house.

Clint watched the bunkhouse for a few moments. Even after Heller had entered there were no lights. Apparently, the man undressed in the dark. He gave Heller time to fall asleep, and Dexter time to do whatever he was doing, before he moved away from the stable and started for the house.

FORTY-ONE

Clint worked his way around to the back of the house. He'd had an angle on the building from his position near the stable and he decided to start at the last place he'd seen the light before Dexter went upstairs. He approached the back door and was able to force it open with a minimum of noise. As he had suspected, he found himself in the kitchen.

He waited a while for his eyes to adjust to the darkness, and also to just listen and see if anyone was moving around inside the house. When he could see fairly well he took a quick look at the room. It was so clean you would think that no one ever used it. He walked around, hesitant to leave the room because Dexter must have gone there for some reason before going to bed.

And then he saw them, oddly illuminated by moonlight coming through the window. A pair of wooden doors, sitting at an angle on one side of the room, probably leading to a root cellar. Clint had been kept prisoner one time for three days in a root cellar. He knew that some of them were as big as rooms, and could even be lived in for a while.

He tried them and found them locked. There had to be a key around somewhere. Eventually, he found one, hanging from a nail on a wall. He fitted it into the lock and the door opened.

It was pitch dark and there was no chance of there being any light down there for his eyes to adjust to. He groped along the wall to one side, and then to the other, and his fingers finally brushed a lamp. He grabbed it and knew he was going to have to take the chance of lighting it.

He stepped down two steps before he lit it, hoping that would keep it from lighting the entire kitchen. When the lamp was going he could see there were seven or eight steps down, and then a hard-packed dirt floor. He started down, wanting to call out but deciding to remain silent as long as he could.

He reached the bottom and used the lamp to light the recesses of the room. In one corner he saw her, tied up, her head hanging forward. Her hair was a tangled mess and now he could smell the smoke in her hair and on her clothes.

"Ramona?" he said.

He moved toward her as she moved her head, then lifted it, squinting against the light.

"Cl—" she started, but she had very little voice.

He looked around the room and saw several canteens in one corner. When he lifted one he found it was full. For some reason, Dexter was hoarding water down here. Clint wondered if the man was expecting some sort of attack. The walls seemed to be lined with canned goods.

He went to Ramona, tilted her head back, and gave

her a little bit of water, just enough to wet her mouth and lips.

"Clint," she said, finally, "thank God."

She leaned against him as he reached behind her to untie her hands, and then did the same for her feet. She slumped and he caught her before she could fall.

"Have you been here the whole time?" he asked.

She nodded.

"Ever since the fire," she said. "Ricks brought me here, and I heard him and Dexter fighting . . . over me."

"I guess Dexter won."

"Clint . . . Art?"

"He's dead, Ramona," Clint said. "I'm sorry."

"I—I knew," she said, "I was just . . . hoping—"

"Come on," he said, "we have to get you out of here."

He pulled her to her feet, but her legs failed her.

"I can't walk."

And he had left his horse a half a mile away.

"We'll have to walk you around a bit down here, try to work some strength into your legs. Come on."

"W—what if they catch us?"

"We'll just have to get out of here before they do."

He started to drag her around, her legs for the most part just dragging.

"H—How did you know . . . I was here?"

"I guess I suspected from the beginning," he said. "If I'd done something, then we could have got you out of here earlier. Instead, we went traipsing all over trying to catch up to Ricks and the others, thinking you were with them?"

"W—with them?"

"We thought they'd taken you," Clint said.

"W—what happened . . . to them?"

"They're all dead."

"Good," she said, with feeling. "They deserved it."

"Did they, uh, try to—"

"No," she said, "Ricks wouldn't let them. He . . . remembered me from another time."

"You don't need to explain anything to me, Ramona. Come on, get your feet under you!"

"I can't," she said, and he had to give her credit. She tried, but she couldn't seem to do it.

"Why didn't you keep moving around down here?" he asked.

"I didn't want to," she said. "I—I didn't expect to be rescued. I just . . . wanted to die."

"Well," Clint said, "you still might get your wish. Here, sit back down."

He put her back where he'd gotten her from and then stood up and stared down at her.

"We're going to need a horse for you," he said. "You'll have to wait here while I get one.

"But—how will you do that without getting caught?"

"Good question," he said. "I guess we'll know the answer soon."

FORTY-TWO

Clint left Ramona in the root cellar with the lamp while he went out the back door and made his way to the barn. He had to wait inside until his eyes got used to the darkness, because he couldn't risk lighting a lamp. There were several horses in stalls and he picked a small, gentle-looking mare for Ramona, and then started looking for a saddle. He finally found one that looked old but usable and put in on the mare. Now the trick was to walk her to the back door of the house without being heard or seen.

He went to the doors of the barn and looked out. The bunkhouse was still dark, as was the house. He talked to the mare a bit, stroked her neck, and then started walking her toward the house. They were out in the open with no cover for what seemed a long time, and he was ready for anything. The only thing he wasn't ready to do was leave Ramona behind. She'd spent days inside that root cellar, already, and he was determined to get her out and to town. Once that was done she could tell the sheriff everything that happened. Maybe Tom Champagne didn't want it to happen, and maybe the town couldn't afford for it to happen, but Pete Dexter was going away for what happened to Art Dwyer.

Clint walked slowly, not wanting to cause the horse to make too much noise. Even though the steps they were taking sounded incredibly loud to him. He didn't know how many of Dexter's men—if any—were willing to kill for their boss, but finding him on the property, apparently stealing a horse, any one of them would probably take a shot at him.

Finally, he and the horse reached the safety of the house. He walked it to the back door and tied it off, then went back inside. The kitchen was still dark, but he could see the light coming from the root cellar. He went to the steps and walked down.

"Ramona?"

"Here," She came out of hiding. "I heard you, but didn't know who it was."

"Well," he said, "at least you were able to get to your feet to hide. Come on, I've got a horse outside for you."

"Only one?"

"Mine's a half a mile from here," Clint said. "I'll put you on this horse and walk it away from here. Once we're far enough we can ride double to where mine is waiting. After that we'll head for town."

"And after that?" she asked. "What do I do after that? Now that Art is gone?"

"I don't now, Ramona," Clint said. "I only know that we have to get away from here before we can think about anything else. Come on."

He put his arm around her and led her up the stairs, leaving the lamp behind. He didn't want to take the time to douse it, and lock the doors of the root cellar behind them. He just wanted to get out of there.

Once outside he boosted her up onto the horse. He took the reins and started walking the animal. He tried to think of a different route that wouldn't take them out into the open, but any other way would simply add distance, and right now the shortest distance was more important.

"Ramona, listen," he said. "This is important. If we're spotted, if there's any trouble I'm going to smack this horse on the rump. You ride into town and get the sheriff, understand?"

"But . . . what about you?"

"I'll have to keep anyone from following you, and then hold them off until you come back with help."

"But you'd never be able to hold them all off."

"You let me worry about that," he said. "Now, we have to be very quiet, so no more talking."

He walked the horse around the house to the front, and then across the open space between the house and the barn. He kept looking both ways, at the house, at the bunkhouse, waiting for a telltale light. However, when the trouble came there was no light to give it away.

The door of the bunkhouse opened and a man staggered out. His intention was clear, as he was already opening the front of his pants.

"Shit," Clint said under his breath.

The man looked up, saw them and squinted, then said, "Hey, what're ya doin'?"

But he didn't shout it. He was puzzled, but not alarmed. Clint thought quickly, came up with several scenarios and discarded them in the span of a minute. In the end he stuck to his original plan.

"Head for town and don't look back," he said to Ramona, and then slapped the horse's rump as hard as he could with his hand. The horse leaped forward before Ramona could say a word.

"Wha—?" the man said, still puzzled.

Clint closed the distance between him and the man and cold cocked him with his gun. The man started to fall, and Clint caught him. He started to drag him around the side of the bunkhouse and thought he was in the clear until he heard the other voice, speaking low.

"Harry? That you? What'd you do, you dope, fall down? Not supposed to drop your pants until ya— Harry?"

Whoever was speaking came out the door and stopped short when he didn't see Harry.

"Hey, Harry?" Louder now, but still not loud enough to wake the entire bunkhouse.

"Here," Clint called out in a loud whisper.

"Ah, what're ya doin'?" the other man called. "Pissin' against the side of the bunkhouse. The boss won't like tha—"

As the speaker came around the corner Clint treated him the same way he'd treated Harry. He caught the man as he fell and dragged him over to where Harry was lying. That done he stopped and listened . . .

FORTY-THREE

When somebody lit a lamp in the bunkhouse he knew he was in trouble. He had two choices. He could run, or he could meet them head-on as they came out, gun in hand. How many would come out to see what was going on? How many of those would have guns in their hands? And how long could he hold them off?

He decided to run, a decision he immediately regretted, but then who makes the right decision every time? Someone coming out of the bunkhouse saw him and yelled, "Hey, who's that guy?"

Clint ran to the barn as more men came out of the bunkhouse, including the foreman, Bart Heller.

"What's goin' on?" he shouted.

"Hey, what happened to Harry and Dave?"

"Are they alive?" Heller asked.

"Yeah, but they're out cold."

"Hey, boss, some guy ran into the barn."

"Did you get a look at him?"

"Naw, it's too dark."

"Okay," Clint heard Heller shout, "cover the barn,

front and back, and don't let him out—and for chrissake, get your guns."

"Where you goin'?" somebody yelled.

"To get Mr. Dexter."

Clint wondered how long it would take Ramona to get to town and how long it would take Champagne to get back here—and when he arrived, what could one more man do? What were the chances that the lawman would stop to deputize some men to come out here with him? And if he did stop to do that, would Clint be dead by the time he and his men did arrive?

More and more it was looking like he made the wrong move running into the barn. It also looked like he was going to have to get himself out of this mess.

Pete Dexter came running downstairs to see who was pounding on his front door.

"What the hell—" he shouted, as he opened it.

"Boss, we got a man trapped in the barn."

"Who is it?"

"I don't know for sure," Heller said, "but I can guess."

"Adams? What would he be—wait—"

Dexter turned and ran into the house. Heller followed him into the kitchen. Where Heller lit a lamp and then gaped at the open doors of the root cellar.

"She's gone."

"Who's gone?" Heller had no idea what his employer was talking about. Dexter had not let anyone know that he had Ramona in the house, except for Hal Ricks, who had brought the woman to him.

"What's goin' on?" Heller shouted.

"If that's Adams in the barn," Dexter said, "I want him dead, Heller. Do you hear me? I want him dead tonight!"

FORTY-FOUR

Clint peered out the front doors of the barn and saw five or six men fanned out there. He moved to the back, where there was a single door. He was able to peek through a crack, and saw a similar line of men there. None of them seemed about to move forward. Apparently, their orders were still just to keep him inside.

There were two horses in the barn. He assumed that one of them belonged to Pete Dexter. One of his options was to jump on one of these horses and ride out the front doors. Maybe he'd get through the line of men without a shot being fired. It was more likely, however, that they would shoot and he'd be hit once, maybe twice. Even after that, maybe he'd be able to hang onto the horse until he got to town and found the doctor.

Or he'd be hit more than twice and die.

He went back to the front to look out. The men had lit torches, which were lighting up the area pretty well. He was still waiting for Heller to come back, maybe with Pete Dexter in tow. By now the rancher must have discovered that Ramona was gone.

And then there they were, both of them standing side by side.

"Adams!"

That was Dexter. Clint decided not to answer right away. Let the man wonder for a while.

"Come on, Adams," Heller shouted. "Who else could it be but you?"

Good point, Clint thought.

"Dexter," he called back, "Ramona is on her way to town. She'll be back with the sheriff."

"So?" Dexter called. "You're trespassing on my land, Adams. I'm within my rights to kill you."

"You wouldn't be killing me because I'm trespassing," Clint said. "You'd be doing it to shut me up. But you can't shut Ramona up. What are you going to do about her?"

"That will come later," Dexter said. "Right now I have to deal with you."

"I'm sure Heller knows you had your neighbor, Art Dwyer, killed," Clint called back. "In fact, I'm sure he hired it done for you—but do your men know about it? How many of them know they're working for a murderer?"

Clint was looking outside when he said it, and he saw a few of Dexter's men exchange glances. He wondered if the men in the back of the barn could hear him as well.

"My men are loyal, Adams," Dexter said. "You won't get them to believe lies. Now, why don't you come out of there and we'll go and see the sheriff about this. I'm sure you'll only spend a little time in jail for trespassing and for breaking into my house."

"Come on, Dexter," Clint said. "I wasn't born yesterday. As soon as I step out these doors you'll shoot me down—but I do think that you and Heller will have to do it. These men hired on as ranch hands, not as gunmen."

"You're talking nonsense, Adams," Dexter said. "Nobody is going to shoot you."

"Okay," Clint said, "let me think about that for a while . . ."

As Clint lapsed into silence Dexter said to Heller, "Open fire on him as soon as he steps out."

"Right," Heller said. "You boys hear the boss?"

"Shoot him when he comes out?" one of the men asked. "B—but didn't Mr. Dexter just tell him we wouldn't do that?"

"Do you work on this ranch, Munson?" Heller asked.

"Well, sure, but—"

"You want to keep workin' here, you'll do as you're told," Heller went on loudly. "And that goes for the rest of you. Understand?"

"Well," Munson said, "no, I don't. What's he talkin' about Mr. Dwyer? We heard his ranch was raided. Why's he sayin' Mr. Dexter hired it done."

"The man is a liar," Dexter said. "He's got it in for me."

"But . . . why?"

"I don't know, Munson," Dexter said. "Maybe you'd like to go into the barn and ask him?"

"No, sir," Munson said, "I don't think so." He turned to the man next to him and said, "Who is this guy in the barn, anyway?"

"All I heard was 'Adams,' " the man said, with a shrug.

"Are you ready to shoot down somebody you don't know?" Munson asked.

"He's trespassin'," the man said.

"He's trapped in the barn with almost fifteen of us out here," Munson said. He looked at the man on his other side. "What about you?"

"I don't know," the other man said.

"The fella in the barn is right about one thing," Munson said. "I didn't hire on as no gunman."

"Munson!" Heller said. "Shut up."

"I'm sorry, boss," Munson said, "but I ain't ready to shoot a man down without knowin' why."

Heller walked over to Munson and backhanded him across the face. The blow knocked the smaller man onto his back.

"You'll take orders or get off this ranch."

Munson wiped his hand across his mouth, then rolled over, got to his feet, and brushed himself off.

"Then I guess I'm out of here," he said, and walked away.

Clint watched this through the space between the two front barn doors.

"What's the matter, Dexter?" he called out. "Having trouble with some of your men?"

He watched the man called Munson walk off, with some of the others looking after him.

All they needed was a little push to walk away, too.

FORTY-FIVE

"Tell your men about the woman, Dexter!" Clint shouted.

"Get him out of there!" Dexter hissed at Heller.

"Tell them about Dwyer's wife and what you did to her."

"Get him out!" Dexter almost shouted.

"He has a gun," Heller said. "I told you I wouldn't go against him with a gun."

"Damn you—"

"How do you suggest I get him out?"

"Tell your men how you kept a woman locked up in your root cellar!" Clint shouted.

Clint could see Dexter's men looking at each other.

"Burn him out," Dexter said.

"What?"

"Burn it!"

Heller shrugged and said, "It's your barn."

Heller grabbed a torch from one of the nearest men and threw it up into the open hayloft.

"What the hell—" one of the men shouted.

"What's he talkin' about the woman?" another shouted.

"Munson was right," a third man said. "We didn't hire on for this."

As smoke began to full the barn Clint saw two, then a third man holster their guns or—if they didn't have a holster—simply lower the gun and walk away.

"He's crazy," someone said. "He's burnin' his own barn."

What was left of the men were milling about now, wondering what to do.

"Dexter!" Clint shouted. "I'm coming out. It's you and me and your foreman, Dexter. I've got no beef with your men. They don't have any use for a man who keeps a woman a prisoner in his home."

"Shut him up!" Dexter shouted.

Heller just stared at him.

The flames were spreading throughout the barn. The horses were panicking and Clint knew he couldn't leave them in there. He went and got them and struggled to get them to the front door. When he kicked the doors open the horses ran out, and he followed. The smoke had started to sting his eyes and the fresh air felt good in his lungs.

Some of Dexter's remaining men ran after the horses, others just fell by the wayside to watch now. Clint was facing Heller and Dexter.

"I'm out of this, Adams," Heller said. "It's between you and him."

"No, you're in it as deep as he is, Heller," Clint said. "You killed the deputy."

"He told me to."

"I don't care."

"Wait, Adams," Dexter said. "we can talk. We can make a deal."

"Can you bring Art Dwyer back to life?" Clint asked. "That's the only deal I'll listen to."

"That's crazy!"

"This is it, Dexter."

"I have money!" Dexter shouted. "This isn't fair!"

"What is?" Clint asked and drew his gun.

FORTY-SIX

For the third—and probably last—time Clint awoke wedged between two beautiful bodies.

The arrival of Tom Champagne and Ramona at the Dexter ranch the night before had staved off any trouble Clint might have had from the ranch hands there after killing their foreman and boss. Instead, everybody got together to try and save the barn.

Clint had returned to town beat, and when he got to his room he discovered Monica and Rachel already waiting in his bed. Luckily, they were asleep, and he was able to crawl in between them—just barely. They parted as he slid in, and then closed around him, which was certainly nothing to complain about.

After Ramona told Sheriff Champagne her story Clint had no trouble with the killing of Heller and Dexter. Adding to that was the fact that the three men in jail had finally admitted to being hired by Heller—once they were shown his body to identify.

When Clint awoke he tried to slide out from between the two women, but they wouldn't have it.

"You got in without waking us up," Monica said, as she closed her legs around his waist.

"You're not gettin' out that way, too," Rachel said, sitting on his chest.

Clint was having breakfast with Tom Champagne and Ramona, but he was going to be late.

"You're late," Champagne said.

"I was saying good-bye."

Ramona smiled at him as he sat down.

"How are you doing?"

She shrugged.

"I still have a ranch to run," she said. "If the army doesn't take away the contract I should be busy."

"They won't take it away," Clint said. "A contract is a contract with those people."

"I hope you're right," she said. "I'll need something to keep me occupied."

The way Tom Champagne was looking at Ramona, Clint didn't think she'd have any trouble.

"What are you going to do?" she asked him.

"Well," he said, "I've got to give you back that steel-dust I've been using. I don't like him."

"You can have any horse on the grounds, Clint," Ramona said.

"Oh, I'll pay for it—"

"Not after saving my life, you won't," she said. "I think that's payment enough for anyone, don't you, Sheriff?"

"Definitely."

"Well," Clint said, "I'll come out and have a look."

He didn't think he was going to find Duke's permanent replacement out there, but he needed something to get him to his next stop—wherever that was.

"I have to be going," Ramona said, standing up. "I have to visit Art's grave, and then get out to the ranch to see if I have any more men working there."

"After last night," Clint said, "I think there might be some men looking for jobs."

"After last night," she said, "I think I'll hire them." She put her hand on Clint's shoulder. "I'll see you out there." To the sheriff she said, "Thank you for breakfast, and everything."

"You let me know what I can do, Ram—uh, Mrs. Dwyer."

"You can call me Ramona, Sheriff."

"And you can call me Tom."

"I'll be seeing you, Tom."

Both men watched her walk out, and then Clint looked at Sheriff Tom Champagne.

"Been in love with her long?"

"Since she first got to town," Champagne said. "It shows?"

"To me, it does," Clint said. "You might have to convince her, though."

"I will," the lawman said, "after a respectable amount of time goes by. It's gonna be good for the town if she can keep Art's operation going."

"Somehow," Clint said, to the lovesick sheriff, "I think she's going to be good for this town in more ways than one."

Watch for

THE LYNCHED MAN

222nd novel in the exciting GUNSMITH series
from Jove

Coming in June!